THE ALIEN'S ENCOUNTER

GRACE KENSINGTON

1

———

"There was nothing left, Maxim," Athan said, his voice soft but leading as if he were trying to tell Maxim something without actually putting it into words. "I ran to the place where he had been, but there was nothing. There was no sign that he had ever been there at all."

"Where did they go?" Maxim asked. He was struggling to keep his voice calm, but he knew that there was a slight tremble in it from the anger that was beginning to course through his veins. "Where did the winged warrior and the silver-haired warrior go after my father disappeared?"

Athan shook his head.

"They walked away. They said nothing to me."

"And you just let them go?" Maxim asked.

"What was I to do, Maxim? We were in the middle of a battle. It felt like the world was crashing down around us and I had just watched my dearest friend, the man who I believed was going to save our kind and bring back the peace and the strength that we once had, die in front of me."

"You didn't watch him die," Maxim said. "You watched him get destroyed."

"And with him went all of my hopes for the future. You don't understand what it was like for us. None knew of the Order, so there was nowhere that we could turn for help to stand up against the corruption that your father was beginning to uncover. We were invisible in an already invisible world."

"He had a name," Maxim growled.

Athan looked at him strangely.

"What?" he asked.

"He had a name!" Maxim roared. He felt Ivy's hand touch his back. "Everything was taken from him. Don't take his name from him, too."

Athan looked at him for a long, still moment.

"Aegeus," he said calmly. "You don't understand, Maxim," he repeated, seeming to slow his words slightly as he said them to make sure that Maxim heard and understood each one completely.

"Of course I don't understand!" Maxim said. "How was I supposed to understand anything when all of this was kept from me for all these years? I was just a child when he died, Athan. I spent my entire life wondering what happened to him and what possibly could have led to him dying in such a way that we weren't even able to bury him so that my mother and my brother and I could go to visit him. Now I find out that my entire life not only you, my father's most trusted friend, but my mother knew that there was more to it and just never told me. How do you expect me to understand anything when you don't even give me the chance to know everything?"

"I'm sorry," Athan said. "I did what I thought was right at the time. Aegeus didn't tell me what he had planned for that battle, or even what he found out. I never had the chance to find out everything, and I didn't know what else to tell your mother. Ellora knew that it had to do with the Order, and I know that she knew about the Klimnu. We never talked about it since, and I don't know how much he told her, but I know that she did know about the group turning and about your father's determination to overcome them. Have you asked her what else she knew?"

"Yes, I've asked her. She won't tell me anything. She hates that I even know about the Order and she doesn't want anything to do with it. Even after all of these years she is still afraid to even talk about them. What could possibly have happened that would make her afraid of a group that is still anonymous for something that happened more than two decades ago?"

"The Order is powerful, Maxim. More powerful than Aegeus ever let you know. I know that you have memories of us talking and may remember much of what your father told you and showed you, but that is not everything. He kept so much of it from you because he knew that you were still so young and that you wouldn't be able to handle it yet. He didn't want to put the responsibility of that knowledge on you."

"Why not?"

"The Order doesn't discriminate. The fact that you were just a boy doesn't mean anything to them. If they were to find out that you had known about the Order and anything that we did, it would not just be Aegeus's life that would be in danger."

"Why would he choose to be a part of a group like that? Why would you?"

"It's not a choice. The Order is not something that a man chooses, it is something that chooses him, and if you do not answer that call, you are giving up your life and likely the lives of your family. This is a tradition that has persisted well beyond history. As long as there have been Mikana, there has been the Order. Much of what it has done has been good. Our men have protected the clan and the planet in ways that others will never know. But in every fight for good there is always the potential for evil. It is up to those who still believe in the good and who are strong enough to resist the temptations of the darkness to stand up and fight.

That is what your father did. Aegeus believed very strongly in the good of the Order. Even though there were aspects of it that were harsh and frightening, he was committed to all of the good that it had done and all of the good that he believed it could still do. He dedicated himself to not allowing the Klimnu to overtake the Order and transform it the way that they had transformed themselves. Had they succeeded, the Klimnu would have power beyond your imagination. They would have been able to take over all of Uoria and the rest of the species of this planet would be their slaves, even the Mikana. Those who didn't comply would have been forcibly transformed and would either allow the potential within themselves to build up until they were fully Klimnu and went along with what the rest of the army wanted, or they would live out their lives tortured by what they had become. Your father's death might not have eradicated the Klimnu from Uoria, but that sacrifice did prevent them from being able to take over the Order. When he died, the battle raged harder and the men who had once stood beside him fought in his name.

We fought against those who were once our brothers, Order against Order, fighting until they all lay dead and we could return home with only the knowledge that we had done what we could. There was no hero's welcome for us. The clan went along with their lives just as they had before, quiet and unassuming, unaware of everything that had happened. And that is exactly what we had wanted. Our reward was seeing those who didn't know about the Order continuing on as if nothing was strange, nothing was out of place. Those families who had lost people in the battle created stories to explain their loss, and life went on, just as Aegeus and the others would have wanted."

Rage filled Maxim and he felt himself lurch toward Athan before Ivy grabbed onto him and eased him back down into his seat.

"You think that this is what he would have wanted?" Maxim demanded. "He would have wanted for his family to have no idea what happened to him, and to spend our entire lives missing him and wondering if there was anything that we could have done to help him. He would have wanted for us not to be able to even go to the side of his grave and pay our respects to him, or just visit with him in the only way that we would ever be able to again? You think that he would have wanted to give up his life only to have the Klimnu come back and continue to ravage an already destroyed planet?"

"The planet hasn't been destroyed, Maxim."

"What about the badlands? How about all of the Denynso who never made it out of the compound they half abandoned? What about Loralia's kind? She is the only one left. And the winged warriors? No one even knew that they ever existed. Where are they now? What happened to them?"

"The Klimnu didn't do all of that," Athan said.

"Then who did? And even if the Klimnu wasn't responsible for everything that has happened, they are still what started it, and are still what continues all of the hate and division and violence on this planet."

"There are no more Klimnu," Athan told him.

"Yes, there are," Maxim said. "They are here. They are inside each and every one of us. The potential to become those creatures is just waiting inside each of us to take the wrong step, to feel the wrong thing, and to fall under the wrong influence."

"As long as we don't come into contact with the toxins that dissolve our skin, we can't transform."

"Do you really think that, Athan? Do you really believe that the transformation of the Klimnu was about some flowers?"

"That's what started it," he said, sounding slightly defeated.

"If that is what you truly believe, that the Klimnu happened just because their skin reacted to a plant, you are not what I thought you were, or what my father thought you were."

Maxim's hands felt cold and shaky as he stood up. He looked down at Ivy and she stood up beside him.

"Maxim," she said gently, but he held up a hand to stop her.

"We're leaving," he said. "At least I am. I can't stay here and listen to this anymore. I'd like to have you with me, but I won't force you. You can stay if you wish."

Ivy shook her head and reached up to touch his face gently.

"No," she said, her voice sounding slightly tremulous. "I'll come."

Out of the corner of his eye Maxim saw Ivy look at Athan and Athan give her a pained expression in return. Maxim felt heaviness in his chest and belly, but he couldn't force himself to sit down again and listen to more of what the man had to say. He knew that Athan knew more about the last days and moments of his father's life than he did, and that he would be the one that might be able to help him to uncover what had really happened, but he couldn't bear to listen any longer. What Athan was telling him was just too painful, and infuriating in a way that he couldn't explain. He knew Aegeus. Even though he had been just a child when his father had died, Maxim could remember enough of him that he knew that this is not what he would have wanted for his family or for the rest of the planet. There was more to his disappearance in that battle than just an instant and complete decimation. And Maxim knew that it had something to do with the soldiers that flanked him when he walked onto the field.

2

———

"Maxim, please slow down," Ivy called, rushing as quickly as she could to try to catch up with him as he walked in long, aggressive strides away from Athan's house.

"I'm sorry," he said, pausing and turning around so that she could get to him.

He reached out to her and Ivy curled into his arms, resting her head on his chest and sighing at the sound of his heart beating beneath his tunic. The smell of his skin rose up to her and she let her eyes close so she could focus completely on the presence of him. He pressed a kiss to the top of her head.

"I'm sorry," he said again, but this time it didn't sound like he was just apologizing for rushing out of Athan's house and away from her.

"You don't have any reason to be sorry," Ivy answered, turning her head so that she could touch a kiss to the expanse of skin revealed by the open ties of his tunic. "No one knows what you are going through and no one, including you, would know how to react in a situation like this. How could you expect to know what to say or do? You didn't even know that any of this was happening or that it had happened, and now you are having to face it all. I can only imagine how overwhelming and upsetting that is."

"I just wish that there was something else that I could do."

"What do you mean?"

"Like you said, I feel so overwhelmed. I feel like there's nothing that I can do. I talked to my mother, and she doesn't want anything to do with any of this. She is completely content to just go on living her life thinking the exact same things that she has been thinking this whole time and not for a moment worry about anything else, or even consider that there could be more to it than what she thinks."

"It might just be too hard for her, Maxim."

"What do you mean?"

"Your father was everything to her. She loved him with her whole being and when she found him she thought that she would be spending her entire life with him. She believed that they would have children, watch those children grow up, enjoy playing with their grandchildren, and just continue throughout life until they faded away together. Never could she have imagined that she would be left so suddenly and with two sons to raise on her own."

"How do you know that?" he asked.

Ivy pushed back so that she could look up at him, her eyes meeting his so that he could see the look on her face as she gazed at him.

"Because that is how I feel about you."

Maxim pulled her closer and rested his cheek against the top of her head, exhaling deeply.

"I guess you're right," he said. "Now that I have you I

couldn't imagine a single second without you. I don't know what I would do if you were suddenly taken away from me."

"Exactly. The suffering that she went through having to mourn your father while also taking care of you and Kyven, and staying alive herself, and also carrying the burden of keeping the Order and everything that she did know about Aegeus's death a secret was a pain that I don't even want to begin to think about. When you ask her about it and you try to get her to tell you what she might know about the Order, or even bring up things that she might now know about your father's death and try to get her to confront them, you are not just putting her at risk because of what she shouldn't know. You are also forcing her to relive those moments without him. I'm not saying that it has gotten easy for her to live without your father, or that she doesn't still miss him and wish that he was here with her, but I'm sure that it is not as fresh and raw as it was when it first happened. She has learned to go about her days and her nights without him. She has learned to think her own thoughts and to consider herself as her own person rather than thinking in terms of herself and your father together."

"She's right, Maxim.

Ivy pulled away from Maxim's chest and turned sharply to see Ellora walking toward them. Even at the distance she could see tears sparkling in the spectacularly beautiful woman's eyes.

"It is only in the last few years that I have learned to not reach for your father's hand when I am walking through the kingdom, or to roll over in the middle of the night to kiss him when I am having trouble sleeping. It has been so long, and yet to me it is still right here, right now. I am just beginning to know what it is to have a life without him, and when you came back here and started talking about him, it was like Athan had come to my door all over again. It's not that I don't want to think about Aegeus, because I think about him all the time. There isn't a breath that I breathe that doesn't have a thought or a memory of him in it. But I have learned to live with those thoughts and those memories. They have become as much a part of me as my blood. What you are looking for and the things that you are trying to find out are threatening those thoughts and memories.

It's not that I don't think that there isn't more to this, and it's not that I believe that I know it all, but what you are trying to do is putting everything at risk. If the Order found out, we could all lose our lives. If they don't, I will still lose what I have left of your father. Those are not risks that I am willing to take. I'm sorry if that hurts you in some way, but I just don't see the purpose in any of what you are doing. It won't change anything. It won't bring your father back or heal any of the old wounds."

"But what if it can help prevent further ones?" Maxim asked, taking a step toward his mother.

Ivy caught hold of his hand before he got too far away from her. The emotion in him was still so high and she didn't want him to upset Ellora any more than he already had. She didn't know exactly what was going on or what Maxim had in front of him to discover, but she did know that this was not the moment for him to delve any further into it. Ellora didn't look strong enough to handle any more.

"Where is your brother?" Ivy asked, guiding Maxim back toward her.

Maxim looked at her and then back at his mother, and then back at her.

"I don't know."

"He is showing that woman the rest of the kingdom."

"What is it that you have against her?" Maxim asked.

Ellora shook her head.

"Neither is Ivy," he said.

"Maxim, I don't want to have this conversation."

Ivy could feel her partner tense beside her and reached down to intertwine their fingers. She gave his hand a reassuring squeeze, hoping to offer him some of her strength.

"We should find Kyven," Ivy said softly, holding Maxim close to her side.

"Athan said..."

"We should find Kyven," Ivy repeated,

She knew that Athan had said that Kyven wasn't ready to hear everything that he had told them, but Maxim had already decided that he wasn't going to fully trust Athan. All that they could do was tell Kyven what they had learned so that he would be able to help them in any way that he could. This may be a journey that they would have to take without the guidance of the people who Maxim had loved and trusted the most when he was young, but that only meant that he was going to need to support and encourage of those that he did have even more.

3

—————

"What are you doing?" Samira asked, reaching ahead of her.

Eden laughed and looked over at Zuri who stood on the other side of Samira. Zuri checked the knot on the back of the blindfold that covered Samira's eyes and placed a hand on Samira's back to help guide her down the steps off of Zuri's house. Ero and Pyra were standing at the bottom of the steps to catch hold of her arms and guide her the rest of the way down. When Eden made it to the bottom she offered a kiss to Pyra and smiled up at him.

"Are you sure that Lysander is going to be alright?" he asked.

Eden laughed softly at the roles within their relationship yet again changing. She and her mate went back and forth frequently with how they felt about their son and their protectiveness over him. There were some moments when Pyra wanted his son to be brave and strong and was willing to be a bit more permissive with what he would do, but Eden felt afraid of letting their tiny son out of her sight. At other times Eden would choose an activity or make a choice that she thought was completely safe, and Pyra would be the one who would suddenly be afraid for Lysander's safety. Now that she had asked her grandmother, one of the few family members on Earth who she had a relationship with that was close enough to want to see her much less to trust her with her son, to babysit while she and Pyra attended Samira's surprise birthday party and engagement celebration, it was one of those moments when Pyra was feeling uneasy and unsure

"Lysander is going to be just fine," she reassured her mate. "I spent a lot of my childhood with Gramma. There are no two hands on this planet that I would feel safer putting our son in than hers."

"How old is she?"

Eden laughed again. She had specifically chosen not to introduce her grandmother to Pyra yet. She knew that she would have to eventually, but she felt like it might take a bit of time for her blunt, upfront grandmother to get through the intensive questioning and examination of her mate that Eden was positive was going to come.

"Old," Eden admitted, "but still sharp as a tack. Nothing gets past that woman."

They were now guiding Samira down the slight hill in front of Zuri's house toward the long luxury vehicle that they had rented for the evening. Her footing was unsteady and Ero and Zuri were having to support nearly all of her weight while Eden and Pyra stood behind them ready to catch any of them that happened to topple over before they made it all the way to the vehicle. This entire adventure was just beginning and already Eden was starting to see flaws in the plan.

"So tell me again why it is that you didn't want me to

meet her?" Pyra asked. "If she was so important in your life, wouldn't you want her to meet your mate?"

"Of course I do," Eden said, reaching forward to offer a bit of support to Samira as she tipped precariously backwards for a moment before continuing ahead. "And she is still extremely important in my life. I just haven't been able to see her as often recently for reasons that I am sure that you understand."

"You don't think that she will like me," Pyra said.

Eden looked at him and noticed the saddened look on his face. Even though he would never admit it, Eden had seen over his first few days on Earth that Pyra was not entirely comfortable with being away from his home planet and around so many humans. On Uoria he was accustomed to being extremely important and leading with an unwavering confidence and strength. The rest of the clan admired him and even when he faltered as he did in his leadership of the expedition to the Nyx 23 settlement, they were willing to forgive him and help him to rebuild himself. He was comfortable around his own kind and was accustomed to being engaged in battle with those that he didn't know and didn't understand. He was just starting to get used to the idea of creating true alliances with other species and being able to live and cooperate alongside them.

Being on Earth had forced him into a situation that was unknown and felt, in a way, unsafe. The humans who he had met recognized him as one of the exotic and alluring Denynso warriors who they had studied and been so fascinated with. They didn't, however, know him by name or understand his station within his clan. Eden could see that he was feeling unsure of himself, insecure in the thought that the people around him, who far outnumbered the Denynso who were on Earth, might not appreciate his presence or might not be willing to accept them. He felt judged and scrutinized for the first time in his life and it was making him feel off-kilter.

Eden reached out and rubbed his arm comfortingly.

"It's not that I don't think that she will like you," she said. "In fact, it might be more than I know that she will like you a lot. When my grandmother likes someone, she feels a sort of possessiveness toward them that fairly often results in conversations that are hours and hours long and have very little hope of escape. She will want to know everything about you and Uoria and your kind. She'll want to know how we met and what our relationship is like."

Pyra reached out to hold onto the door to the vehicle that Ero had opened so that Zuri and Ero could guide the still-protesting Samira into the backseat.

"She'll want to know how we met." Pyra asked.

Eden looked at the somewhat terrified look on her mate's face and had to laugh.

"We can just tell her that you were the very first Denynso warrior I saw when I stepped out of the ship on Uoria and that it was love at first sight," she told him.

"So you are going to lie to your grandmother?"

"Do you want me to tell her that I hated you when I first saw you and I tried to get you to leave me alone because I wanted nothing to do with you, but that the king forced me to have you as my guard and protector, which led to you watching me take a shower and then ravishing me?"

"You are going to lie to your grandmother."

"I thought so."

"Come on, guys," Ero called from inside the vehicle. "We have a...." he glanced back at Samira, who was still blind-folded and reaching around the inside of the vehicle from her seat, "...something to get to."

Eden and Prya climbed in and Eden was immediately awestruck by the colored lights and mirrored interior of the vehicle. Plush seats lined all sides and there was enough space for the five of them as well as the rest of the group that they were supposed to pick up along the way. They settled back onto one of the seats and Ero started pouring champagne into glasses and handing them around.

"And you're sure that she won't have a problem with the fact that I'm Denynso?" Pyra asked.

"Absolutely not," Eden told him. "In fact, Gramma was the one who encouraged me the most when I said that I wanted to be a scientist and find out everything that I could about the world. She told me that that wasn't enough. I should set my sights on finding out everything that I could about the universe and beyond."

"And in all the universe, you found me," Pyra said.

Eden reached for the glass of champagne that Ero was holding out to her and raised it toward Pyra.

"Yes," she said with a smile, "and that is more than I ever thought that I would know."

She touched the rim of her glass to his and took a sip. He followed suit, giving a strange look to the glass as he swallowed his first mouthful. Eden remembered then that this was the first time that the Denynso had, had Earth-originated beverages such as champagne. She hoped that it wouldn't impact them the way that it had a tendency of impacting humans. If they all started feeling a bit out of control, there was no way that the human women would be able to rein them in.

4

———

Zyyr leaned back against the curved stone of the wall and closed his eyes, letting the warmth of the sun heat the skin of his face. He wondered if he was ever going to get fully used to the strange weather on this portion of Uoria. He was so used to the weather patterns of the compound and it hadn't occurred to him when he planned on leaving the first time on the quest with Pyra and the other warriors that one of the most challenging things that they would encounter would be the strange and unpredictable weather. A hint of a smile came to his lips as he thought about how strange it was that after everything that they had gone through in the last several weeks that it would be the intensity of the sun, the temperature of the air, and the frequency of the precipitation that would be what would linger with him.

"It is nice to see such a lovely smile on a Denynso warrior."

The sweet voice opened Zyyr's eyes and he found a woman looking down at him from a few feet away. She was the most stunningly gorgeous woman he had ever seen, and for a moment he wondered if he was imagining her. She simply seemed to perfect to exist, but suddenly it occurred to him that she must be one of the notoriously beautiful and entrancing Mikana. Until that moment he had met only the men, but now he saw how the appeal of the man translated into a woman so incredible he couldn't even bring himself to speak.

"Did I bother you?" she asked, sounding concerned and taking a step back.

She was holding a large basket tucked close to her hip and as she moved it started to slip out of her grasp. Zyyr jumped up and rushed forward to help her stabilize it before she dropped it. As he did he forced the expression on his face to look less startled and more friendly.

"No," he finally forced past his lips. "No, you didn't bother me at all. I just didn't realize there was anyone here."

"I was just going to gather some fruit from the orchards," she said by means of explanation for breaking through his private thoughts. "My name is Lila."

She held her hand up in front of her, but Zyyr didn't know what she wanted him to do. He thought of the greeting rituals that he had learned from the humans of the settlement and took her hand, resting her long, slender fingers against his palm so that he could bring the back of her hand to his lips and tenderly touch a kiss to her pale skin. As soon as his mouth touched her skin, his body felt like it lit on fire. Tightness in his belly formed until it was like he was being tied in a knot, and he could feel the front of his pants straining against an erection that was almost painful in its intensity.

It was a strange and overwhelming feeling, something that he had not been prepared to experience. In all of his years he had heard the men of his kind talking about the sometimes excruciating physical and psychological experience of anticipating their mates. They spoke of dealing with days of unbreakable physical desire and a level of aggression and anger that threatened to overcome them. Brothers and best friends had engaged in fearsome fights during these times, the feelings within the man who was close to meeting his intended causing him to nearly tear the other to pieces.

In this moment, however, Zyyr felt absolute peace and calm. Though his body and his mind were telling him with absolute certainty that this woman, this incredible, almost unbearably beautiful woman, was meant to be his, he wasn't feeling any of what he had expected throughout his life. He didn't know what to make of it, but he knew that he wanted very much to continue to enjoy the aura of relaxation and contentment that Lila seemed to create around him.

"You are looking at me strangely again," Lila said, her pretty face scrunching slightly as she looked back at Zyyr with an expression like she was searching within him and trying to understand what was going on in his thoughts.

"I'm sorry," Zyyr said, looking down briefly and giving a short laugh. "I don't mean to look at you strangely. My name is Zyyr."

Lila looked down at her hand and then back at him expectantly.

"I liked the way that you greeted me before," she admitted softly.

Zyyr slowly lifted her hand again and touched his lips to it in another kiss, not taking his eyes away from hers.

"May I come along with you to the orchards, Lila?" he asked.

Lila nodded, her thick waves of dark, glossy hair moving around her shoulders and waist almost like liquid.

"I would like that very much."

Zyyr reached for the basket and she handed it over to him. He realized as he took it that it wasn't empty as he had expected it to be. Instead, it held a piece of red and white fabric draped over something.

"I brought along a picnic lunch," Lila said as if explaining the fabric even though he hadn't asked her about it.

"I'm sorry," he said, feeling suddenly awkward. "I didn't mean to intrude on your picnic."

He started to hand the basket back to her, but Lila smiled and shook her head.

"I brought along enough for the two of us," she said.

"You did?" Zyyr asked, shocked by the revelation.

"Yes," she said simply and started walking.

Zyyr followed her in silence as they walked along the edge of the stone wall that surrounded the kingdom much like the one at the settlement. He noticed as they walked that the wall was belling out. Though he had expected for it to maintain a close and relatively uniform shape like the settlement, this one seemed much larger toward the back, particularly to one side, than in the front. It had appeared relatively small as they approached it first, but now Zyyr realized that it was far, far larger than he had anticipated.

They had walked for several minutes before he saw the orchards. The trees grew in neat, uniform rows, the ground beneath and between them clean and smooth. He paused slightly and stared at the trees, trying to understand their perfect pattern.

"How do they grow like that?" he asked.

Lila turned around and cocked her head at him slightly, a look of questioning on her face.

"What do you mean?" she asked.

"They are in such straight lines and there are no other plants or trees or anything around them."

"It's an orchard," she said as if that explained everything. "Don't you have orchards on your compound?"

Zyyr shook his head.

"No," he told her. "I'll admit that I was not entirely sure what an orchard was when I asked if I could go with you."

"So why did you ask?" Lila asked coyly, glancing down at her feet and then back up at him.

"So that I could spend more time with you," Zyyr said.

She smiled and looked down again briefly.

"An orchard is where we plant trees of a specific kind so that we can grow and harvest their fruit. Where do you get food on your compound?"

"There is a forest," he told her, "and gardens. I have never heard of someone raising trees."

He felt a sense of awe and admiration for these unusual and truly amazing people. He found himself wanting to know more about them, craving a deeper understanding of Lila and her kind nearly as much as he craved her touch. They walked on for a few more yards before Lila stopped again and instructed him to put the basket down. She reached in and pulled off the cloth, revealing that it was a small blanket covering an abundance of food that Zyyr didn't recognize but that looked and smelled delectable.

They settled onto the blanket and Lila began to unpack the basket.

"Why did you bring enough for two people?" Zyyr asked.

He hated to think that she might have had plans to meet someone else in the orchard, but immediately assumed that if she had, she probably would not have been so willing, and even eager, for him to come along with her. Lila looked up at him with a hint of shyness in her eyes and gave him a smile.

"I've been watching you since you first arrived here with the others," she admitted.

"You have?" Zyyr asked, even more surprised by this revelation than he was by the first.

"Yes," she told him. "I noticed that you spend a lot of your time out by the wall, and I wanted to have a chance to talk with you. Was that dishonest of me?"

He smiled at her.

"No. I'm glad that you did."

They spent a few moments eating in silence and then Zyyr noticed that Lila was gazing over the wall with a wistful look in her eyes.

"What are you thinking about?" he asked.

She sighed and looked at him.

"Just...." she trailed off, looked at the wall again, and then back at him, "What is it like out there?"

Zyyr swallowed a bite of a rich, flaky bread that reminded him of something that Ty would have baked, and looked at her quizzically.

"What do you mean?" he asked.

"The planet," she said, leaning toward him. "What is the planet like outside of the kingdom?"

"You've never been outside of the wall?" he asked.

Lila shook her head and sat back, suddenly looking faintly sad.

"No. I've spent my entire life here. It's only the men who are permitted to leave the kingdom at will, and even then they have to be of age before they do. Of course, some do their best to sneak out and do a little exploring. For me, though, my life has been within this boundary. I've always wondered what it was like outside; what I might find and what it would be like to just be able to go anywhere and do anything without having a wall to stop me." She paused and looked down, picking at the last bit of food that she had in front of her as if embarrassed of what she was saying. "I guess you really wouldn't understand that."

Zyyr shook his head and reached out to touch her hand. The feeling of his skin against hers was electrifying, but he concentrated instead on her eyes as they lifted to look at him.

"I do understand," he told her. "Up until the Denynso left the compound only a few weeks ago and found the settlement, we weren't permitted to leave. We spent our entire lives within the boundaries of the compound. The difference is that most of us never even considered the possibility of leaving. I know I didn't. I never even thought about what might be outside of the compound or what it might be like to go to other areas of the planet."

Color splashed across Lila's cheeks and she glanced away from him.

"You must think that I am completely out of my mind or really silly to have thoughts like that," she said softly.

"No," Zyyr told her, tightening his grip on her hand so that she would feel the connection between them and know that he was there, in that moment, with her. "I think you are very brave."

5

———

"**S**urprise!"

Eden held onto Samira's shoulders while Zuri pulled the blindfold away from her eyes, revealing the crowd of people standing in the small bar. A strange conglomeration of birthday and wedding decorations covered the space and Eden noticed that a few of the guests wore shiny metallic birthday hats while others sipped drinks from novelty glasses featuring tiny faux pearl necklaces around the stem and little tulle veils attached to the sides. It was a hilarious, if confusing, combination of the two events that they were celebrating that night.

"What happened here?" Eden asked, leaning toward Zuri as Samira stepped away from them to greet her guests.

"I told Jane and Simran to handle some of the details. I have a feeling that the decorations got delegated to some Denysno and they might have raided a party supply store with only the words "birthday" and "engagement" to go on."

Eden covered her mouth to muffle her laugh and watched as a delighted Samira accepted a bouquet of roses from Ty and got on her toes to kiss him.

"I know that I'm not familiar with all of the traditions and customs of your kind," Ty said, stroking her cheek and gazing at her lovingly, "but the others have been trying to educate me on them so that I can understand what we are celebrating. Tonight I know that we are not just celebrating our plan to come together in marriage, but also the day that you were born. The people who knew you best when you lived here, before you came to Uoria and found me, tell me that your birthday is not something that you celebrated willingly, and many didn't even know when it was. I don't know why that is and I won't ask you, but I do want you to know that this day marks the first of what I hope will be many, many days that I will celebrate the most precious gift that has ever been given to me, and feel unexplainable gratitude that on this day you came into existence."

Eden felt tears forming in her eyes and Pyra's hand came around her waist to pull her closer to him. She rested her head against his arm, taking a moment herself to feel grateful that he was there with her and that she had discovered him. She knew that she had gone through a series of complex and often painful decisions in the days and weeks leading up to meeting him, and if she had made a single one differently, she wouldn't be standing there with him, the feeling of their child still lingering in her arms.

From behind her Eden heard someone say her name. The voice was familiar, but the word sounded surprised, almost shocked. She turned around and saw a woman who she vaguely knew from the university staring back at her.

"Hello, Evangeline," Eden said with a smile.

"It is you," Evangeline said, her voice somewhat powdery now as if the surprise of seeing Eden had taken away all of her energy.

"Yes, it is," Eden said, unsure of what else she should say. "How are you?"

Evangeline just continued to stare at her for several seconds, and then looked up at Pyra.

"Hello," he said, extending an enormous hand toward Evangeline in the handshake gesture that Eden had taught him on their way to Earth. "My name is Pyra. I'm Eden's mate."

"Nice to meet you," Evangeline said.

She turned her questioning gaze back to Eden and then turned away, walking deeper into the party without saying anything else.

"That was strange," Eden said.

Eden accepted a glass of champagne from Zuri as she approached.

"What was strange?" Zuri asked.

Eden brought the rim of the glass to her lips and gestured with her eyes for Zuri to look over toward the bar where she could see Evangeline leaned close to a few other women, whispering animatedly.

"Do you know Evangeline?" she asked.

"No," Zuri said, shaking her head. "Who is she?"

"She is someone who I knew kind of from a distance from working in the lab. Even though I wasn't technically part of the university program, working with Ryan meant that I came into contact with people from the university fairly often. She was one of the women who came into the lab every now and then to share research with Ryan. She just came up to me and acted like she had seen a ghost. She was completely shocked that I was here."

"Why?" Zuri asked.

Eden shrugged.

"I don't know. She didn't really say anything. Just 'it is

you' and then she said hello to Pyra and that was it. She just kind of walked away."

Zuri took another sip of champagne and smiled as Ero wrapped his arms around her waist from behind and pressed a kiss to the side of her neck.

"Come on, everybody," he said. "Ty baked a cake and we are just about to cut it."

The rest of the group started toward the table where Samira and Ty stood, but Eden stayed in place for a moment longer, slowly sipping her champagne and staring at the women at the bar. She knew that there was something more to the strange way that Evangeline had interacted with her. There was something behind the look in the woman's eyes when she saw her and the way that she was conspiring with the other women from the university now. Eden just didn't know what it could be.

6

"I don't understand," Kyven said, turning away from Maxim for a moment and then turning back sharply. "Athan knew all of this all along and never told anybody?"

"He's not supposed to," Maxim said. "This goes even deeper than just the fact that outsiders aren't supposed to know about the Order. This is corruption and conflict within the Order itself. Athan knew that our family was at enough risk because Papa told us about them in the first place. He says that he didn't want to put us in any more danger by telling the truth."

"So he thought it would be better if we just didn't know anything?" Kyven asked, new anger building within him.

It was bad enough that Athan had excluded him from the conversation that he had had with Maxim about their father, but now that he was finding out what it was that they had talked about, a sense of betrayal was forming low in his belly. As the younger brother he had always been the one that felt like he was being left out or that he was always a step behind Maxim. Maxim had always gotten to spend more time with Papa and with their grandfather. He had always been the one to find out more about the Order and what they were doing. When their father had died Kyven thought that the days of him lingering behind his older brother might be behind him, but now he was realizing that it was the same as it had always been.

"I think that there's more that he didn't get a chance to say," Ivy said.

Kyven turned to her and stared into her wide eyes for a moment.

"What do you mean?"

Ivy looked at Maxim tentatively and then back at Kyven.

"Maxim got angry and left before Athan was finished talking. I think that he had more that he needed or wanted to say."

"I couldn't keep listening to him," Maxim said, his voice low and angry. "You know that."

"Why not?" Kyven asked.

"What he was saying about Papa and the way that he died..." Maxim paused and Kyven saw him draw in a breath, "he was sitting there telling me that he never told us what really happened because he felt like this was the way that Papa would have wanted it."

Kyven thought about those words for a moment, letting them sink in so that he could truly process them.

"What if it is?" he finally asked cautiously, knowing that it would infuriate his brother but needing to express the thought.

"What do you mean?" Maxim asked, his voice holding as much anger and ferocity as he thought that it would. "How could it possibly be what Papa would want?"

"You know as well as I do that we were the most important thing in his life. You, me, and Mom. We were everything to him. What if he knew that everything he had found out about the Klimnu and the Order was putting all of us at risk and the only thing that he could do to protect us was to sacrifice his own life."

"Even if that were true," Maxim said. "Why would he not want us to know? Why would he want to make it so that we couldn't even have his body?"

"I don't know that, Maxim." Kyven took a breath and glanced over at Ivy who looked back at him as if she knew what he was going to say and thought that it was exactly what needed to be said. "But you know that Athan does."

Maxim's eyes slid up to Kyven's and he could see an intensity in his brother's glare that spoke of emotion Maxim didn't want to put voice to. Kyven knew then that there was more to what Maxim was feeling than just anger. Just as Kyven was, Maxim was feeling the loneliness, the empty, cold gnawing within him that had started when they learned that their father was dead. Aegeus had been everything to them, more precious than either one of them ever understood. In fact, it wasn't until Kyven knew that he was never going to come back that he really realized just how important his father was to him and how prevalent in his life he really was. He decided to use that now, hoping that it would speak to something inside of Maxim, something buried deep within him that he didn't want to let out; that he didn't even want to admit was there, and could help to push his brother forward on this journey that he had laid out for them.

"Do you remember what it was like when we were younger, Maxim?" Kyven asked, taking a step forward so that he could close the space between himself and his brother. "Do you remember what it was like to spend time with Papa? Can you remember his eyes? The color of his hair?

What it felt like when he scooped us up and gave us those hugs that were like they were never going to end?"

"Yes," Maxim said.

"I don't," Kyven admitted, his voice painful as it pushed through the tightening in his throat. "I miss him every single day and I feel an emptiness in every moment that I know that he should be a part of, but I don't remember those things. I don't remember what he looked like. I don't remember what he smelled like. I don't remember the texture of his skin or the way his hair felt. I know that I should. I know that those memories are somewhere inside me, but it's like they are getting washed away. When we found out that he was dead, it was like part of me had died right along with him. Suddenly I really knew just how much he was a part of our lives and just how important he was to me."

"Me, too," Maxim agreed.

"Up until that moment I never really thought about eating breakfast with him, but that first morning after Athan came and Mom had to tell us what happened, it was like I couldn't stop staring at his chair. Part of me was still waiting for him to come sit down and I felt like I couldn't take a bite until he did."

"It was hard getting dressed without listening to him talking to Mom in the kitchen."

"I couldn't focus on training without his instructions. I couldn't finish any of my chores because I knew that he wouldn't be there to..."

"Rest his hand on the top of our heads and tell us that he was proud of us. I couldn't fall asleep because I couldn't hear them whispering in their bedroom."

Kyven nodded.

"He knew that if he didn't come back from that battle

that he would be leaving a tremendous emptiness in our lives. He knew that it would be difficult enough for us to cope just with not having him around anymore. Maybe he thought that it would be easier for us if we didn't know everything that had happened. What he didn't think about, though, was how long those questions were going to linger with us. He thought that eventually we would forget about him and move on with our lives, and with the thoughts of him would go the questions that we had about the Order. He might have thought that his death would end everything. He had no way of knowing that the Klimnu would continue and that the planet would still be in danger. We have to be the ones to find out what happened and to finish what he started. If we let this go now, the planet will stay at risk and Papa would have died for no reason. There is only so far that we can go on our own. Athan is the closest thing that we have left to Papa, and if he knows more than he has already told you, we need to listen to him."

There was a pause as Kyven tried to gauge his brother's reaction. Maxim's shoulders squared and he took a long, steeling breath.

"I know," he said. "He deserves our memory. He deserves for people to know what happened, not just to him, but to everyone who fought. If Athan is the one who can help us do that, I will trust him."

7

—————

"They are still acting weird," Eden murmured to Zuri as they leaned over the gift table and tried to rearrange the conglomeration of packages, bags, and envelopes into some semblance of order.

"Who?" Zuri asked.

Eden pretended like she was reaching for one of the gifts on the other side of the table so that she could gesture over her shoulder at the women who were still huddled at the bar, whispering conspiratorially and occasionally glancing her way.

"It's like they know something that they aren't telling me. Maybe they are just really surprised to see you with a Denynso like Pyra," Zuri said.

Eden shook her head and gave the women the briefest glance she could so that she could check in on what they were doing without making it obvious that she was looking at them.

"If that was it, wouldn't they be surprised about all of the women? Especially the ones they know better than me, like, oh, I don't know, the bride who they are celebrating tonight and who is marrying one of the warriors?"

She knew that she was starting to lose her grip on her emotions and her self-control, but Eden was starting to feel the same uncomfortable tension around her that she used to feel when she was working in the lab with Ryan. It always felt like there was something going on that she was a part of even though she wasn't privy to what was actually happening. It was a closed, heavy feeling that made her feel like she was being scrutinized from every angle and judged for something that she had nothing to do with and at the same time had contributed to.

Eden was reaching for an envelope someone had placed on top of one of the brightly wrapped gifts when something suddenly occurred to her. She turned so sharply that she brushed that envelope and a stack of others onto the floor, but she didn't take the time to pick them up. Instead, she stalked across the bar toward the women and stepped up close to them.

"You didn't think that I was coming back, did you?" she demanded.

The women looked at her with shocked, somewhat frightened expressions. Evangeline opened and closed her mouth a few times, and turned to stare down into her drink.

"Did you even know that I was going to Uoria? What did he tell you?"

The women continued to stare at her with expressions that told her that she wasn't going to get any information from them. Eden made an angry, exasperated sound and stomped away from the women, looking around the bar for Pyra. She didn't see him, and she didn't have the patience to look around for him. Instead she took several long strides directly over to Zuri and pulled her by her elbow to get her away from a few of the other guests who were starting to crowd around the gift table as if in an effort to convince the birthday girl to start unwrapping.

"If you see Pyra, tell him that if I'm not back here by the end of the party that I will meet him back at the house. He knows how to get to my grandmother's house and he can pick up Lysander on the way."

She started to turn away but Zuri grabbed her hand to stop her.

"Wait," Zuri said, "where are you going? What's wrong?"

Eden shook her head.

"I can't tell you now. I just have to go take care of something."

She pulled out of Zuri's grasp and moved quickly through the rest of the guests at the bar. She had come to the party with the others in the rented car and for a moment she didn't know how she was even going to get across town. Just as she was starting to give up, one of the sleek public transportation vehicles slid into place at the stop across the street. Whispering a few words of thanks at the serendipitous timing, she ran across the street to the stop and jumped into the car. The driver handed her what looked like a small, clear screen and she looked down at it. The image of the city appeared on the glass, showing her where she was and the route that this particular vehicle would take. She moved the image around with her finger and then pressed one of the pulsating red dots to indicate her final destination. She handed the screen back to the driver and he settled it into the port on his dashboard.

Immediately the car shot forward, moving smoothly and comfortably despite its incredible speed. It was only a few moments later that the car pulled up to the low stone bench that Eden had indicated as her destination. She thanked the driver and jumped out of the car. Eden waited until the driver had pulled away to go any further. She didn't want anyone to know where she was going.

Her feet pounded against the pavement as she ran down the empty sidewalk and through a narrow opening in a fence. She hoped that the security codes hadn't changed since she had been gone. She skidded to a stop at an unassuming looking door at the back of a tall building and touched the palm of her hand to the front of the door to access the keypad. In the year that she had been gone there should have been several new codes, but if her assumptions were correct, they wouldn't have changed at all. Not just because she was the only other person who knew of the code, but also the fact that Ryan was just conceited and arrogant enough to make his own birthdate and hiring date the sequence of numbers used to access the labs.

Eden punched the numbers into the keypad and an instant later she heard the low click of the locks within the door releasing. The door slid open slightly and she grabbed the edge to push it completely out of the way. The familiar smell of the laboratory hit her as soon as she stepped into the building and for a moment she felt like she had never left. Everything felt exactly as it had, but she didn't know if that was comforting or if she should be angry. She had suddenly realized exactly why Evangeline and the other women had been so confused, and a little frightened, to see her, and she wanted to know what had compelled Ryan to do it.

The tall heels of her shoes clicked loudly on the polished linoleum floor of the hallway, the sound reverberating off of the walls and making the building feel even more empty than it had when she had first gotten in. She knew, however, that it wasn't empty. Though the section of the hallway that she was walking down was shadowy, but light spilled from under one of the doors at the far end of the corridor and that told her that she was not the only one who had come for a visit in the laboratory late that night. Eden slowed as she got further down the hallway. She stopped and leaned against the wall so that she could take off her shoes and put them aside. The sound was loud enough that if she got much closer to the lit room that anyone inside would be able to hear her approach and she didn't want to give enough advance warning to allow for whatever was going on in there to be stopped before she got there.

Nervousness rolled through her belly as she continued to creep down the hallway. When she was on her way to the lab she had been so filled with anger and frustration that she hadn't thought completely through what she was going to do when she got there. The fears about Ryan that she had expressed to Pyra were building even more intensely inside her now and she wondered if it had been the right decision for her to come here on her own without any true plan of why she was there or what she hoped to accomplish.

She reached the partially open door and took a moment to brace herself. When she stepped in, however, she didn't see anyone. Pausing for a moment to listen for any of the sounds that would indicate that Ryan was somewhere in the back of the lab, she rushed forward to the tall tower of drawers in the back corner. This had been one of Ryan's many strange idiosyncrasies. Though his research had always been devoted to the next advancement and improvements in technology, he had always insisted on taking his notes by hand and keeping hard copies of all of the papers that he submitted. He was never able to give her a clear explanation as to why he did it, but in that moment, she was glad that he did.

Dropping down to her knees in front of the case, she checked to make sure that the lock was the same as it had been when she had left. Again, she wasn't surprised to find that it was. Ryan was too wrapped up in himself to think about something like changing the locks that he had chosen himself. He would simply assume that the plan that he had come up with was going to work perfectly, and when it did there would be no reason for him to change the locks or the codes. A truly arrogant man in everything that he did and thought, Ryan never thought beyond his own goals and plans to imagine that someone might interfere.

Eden typed the series of numbers and letters that she remembered from the many times that Ryan had made her dip into the stacks of paper in the drawers to find pieces of research for his reference. It was truly infuriating to her, and often she felt like that was part of the reason that he did it. She would show him the handheld screens that she used for her own research, the banks of computers that the other researchers used, and he would scoff at her as if she was simply too dumb to understand his viewpoint. Once he took a computer and input all of his notes, performed a few calculations, and utilized a program to coordinate the outline for a project that he was planning simply to show her that he was fully capable of using the same technology, and then erased it all. There was a level of almost psychotic secretiveness to his ways, and a level of meticulousness that showed a mind she was positive was capable of nearly anything.

"Not as capable as mine," she murmured as she pulled an envelope out of the drawer and carried it over to one of the gleaming tables in the center of the room.

She opened the envelope and pulled out the papers. Spreading them out across the table she scanned through them. She didn't understand what they meant and she had read through several of the pages before she glanced at the top and noticed that it was dated for several months after she left. Assuming that these notes were for a project that he had started after sending her away, she pushed them aside and went back to the drawers to pull out another.

This envelope had a scribble on the front that Eden recognized and she felt her heart start pounding as she pulled the older pages out and spread them across the table. Her ears started to ring as she went through the pages line by line. They were so familiar that she felt like she could have recited them word for word as she went. The last time she had read those words, however, she had been the one who had written them. Now, however, they were in Ryan's tightly controlled, precise hand. These notes had been about her own original research into a concept that Ryan had told her was worthless until she had started to delve into it and he realized that she was rushing headlong toward far more impressive advancements than he had been able to accomplish in the time that she had been with him. They had been her thoughts, her innovations, and her research. Now they had been stolen from her.

"You didn't think that I was just going to let all of that research go to waste, did you?"

Eden whipped around so fast that she knocked many of the pages off of the table and across the floor. Ryan was leaning against the doorframe peeling off a pair of gloves as he stared at her.

"How dare you?" Eden said, her hand tightening on the edge of the table as new anger surged through her.

"You know," Ryan said, his voice still sickly smooth,

"when I heard that the university had sent two of their newest shuttles to Uoria so that a group could return here, I had just a moment when I thought that you might be onboard. Then I said to myself, no, that's not possible. You've been gone for a year now. I had very little intention of you surviving the initial arrival on the planet. You see, I am very familiar with the laws of the Denynso, and with their rituals. I knew that they would send a warrior guard who would escort you directly to the king and queen of the compound. I figured that you would try to prove yourself by stealing the blood of the first Denynso warrior you saw and that your impulsiveness would have you dead by sunset. Even if you had somehow managed to get through that first day and none of them had found out about the real reason that you were there, you would only be allowed to be on the planet for six months before they sent you back. There was simply no way that you would be on those ships. Imagine my surprise when I heard that not only did you survive and somehow finagle more than six months out of your stay on Uoria, but that you were one of the group that was returning for a visit."

"Yeah," Eden said, her hand still wrapped tightly around the edge of the table. "It seemed to shock the hell out of Evangeline when she saw me. Why do you think that is?"

She was struggling to keep her voice sounding calm despite the range of emotions coursing through her.

"Perhaps," Ryan said, stepping further into the room, "it's because they didn't even know that you went to Uoria in the first place."

Eden gave him a quizzical look.

"How is that possible? The university knew that I was on that shuttle and they knew where it was going."

"They knew where it was going, yes," Ryan said. "That doesn't mean that they knew that you were on it."

"I don't understand."

Ryan shrugged.

"I suppose that I could have told them that you were going as part of the university exchange program or that you were doing specialized research for me. That might have made it easier for them to understand why I requested a commission of a shuttle and hired my own staff rather than utilizing members of the actual university flight program."

"What?" Eden gasped, taking an involuntary step back.

"That was the beauty of this whole plan. You had spent just enough time working with people from the university that if you had mentioned to anyone that you were going to be going to Uoria, they would automatically assume that you were going as part of the university exchange program without me even having to tell them. Then if they questioned it as not making sense, I could honestly say that I had never been the one to say that you were part of the program, and instead that you were doing some research for a project that I was spearheading for the university."

"That's a lie," Eden said.

"Of course it is," Ryan said with a laugh. "The thing is, I didn't have to tell them either one of those things. Instead, I commissioned the shuttle, I hired the crew, and I set it up so that it looked like an approved visit, even going so far as to contact Uoria and make sure that the Denynso knew that you were coming to perform scientific research."

"You never intended on me coming back," Eden said.

Even though she had already known it, now that Ryan was confessing that the purpose of sending her to the planet was to kill her, the reality was hitting her harder.

"Oh, I never intended it, no," Ryan said. He was within

just a few steps of her now and Eden felt her heart pounding even harder in her chest. "I figured that you would be dead within hours of getting to the planet. That's why I told the women that you had joined an exploration crew for one of the string of planets that were recently discovered on the edge of the fourth galaxy and weren't planning on returning to Earth any time soon."

"And why would I do that?" she asked.

"Because you were so devastated when I rejected your advances, of course," Ryan said, looking particularly proud of himself.

"Excuse me?"

"Well, Eden," Ryan said, running his fingers along the table in a way that made Eden's skin crawl, "everyone around here knows just how crazy you are about me. It's so obvious, and I'm sure that my lunchroom stories didn't hurt the matter. You spent all those long hours helping me in this quiet, isolated laboratory, all the while your heart longing for me and your imagination running wild with a blissful imagined relationship between the two of us. You convinced yourself that one day I would sweep you off your feet and you would no longer be my assistant, but my wife." He gave a deep, whimsical sigh and Eden felt her stomach lurch. Ryan turned a sharp look back to her. "It is completely understandable that when I arrived at the laboratory one night to find you naked and waiting for me on one of my tables, ready to give your body to me and proclaim your love, and I had to let you down gently that you were out of your mind with grief. You just couldn't take the humiliation or the thought that you were going to have to go through the rest of your life pining for me, tortured because your subpar scientific understanding and lack of vision were going to force you to remain in my laboratory as my assistant for the remainder of your career."

"Subpar scientific understanding?" Eden said back to him, keeping her voice low to stop herself from screaming at him. "Lack of vision? These notes are all mine!" she said, gesturing at the papers around her. "I came up with these concepts and designed the experiments. I did the research. You were so busy obsessing over having Denynso blood so that you could weaponize it that you lost all of your focus on any of your actual work."

"And how amazing it would have been if you were able to get that blood for me," Ryan said. "I thought of that, you know. I didn't want to leave anything to chance, so I thought about the possibility that you would actually be able to integrate yourself into the Denynso population enough that you could somehow get the blood and smuggle it back to me. Then I would have exactly what I have always wanted, but I could never let anyone know that it had been you who had gotten the blood." His look grew darker. "Just like I can't let anyone know anything now."

Before Eden could really process what was happening, Ryan lunged toward her. He grabbed her around the neck, tackling her to the ground and pinning her down with his knee in the center of her chest.

"What are you doing?" She managed to gasp out.

"I can't let you tell anyone what you know. I know that you were planning on going to my superiors to report me. I also know that given two seconds you would tell them that this research was yours and why I sent you to Uoria. I just can't let that happen." He tightened the grip on her throat and ground his knee deeper into her chest. "I have too much left to do. You could have been a help, but I'm going to have to just do it without you."

Eden refused to give Ryan the satisfaction of dominating her. She brought her hands up to his chest and shoved with all of the strength that she could gather into her arms. Ryan look stunned as the force of her shove sent him tumbling back off of her.

"What would you tell the people from the university?" she asked, scrambling to her feet. "You have gotten yourself into a hole that you are never going to be able to dig yourself out of, Ryan. They are going to figure out that you lied to the university, you lied to the Denynso people, and that you lied to everyone in the scientific community. They know that I'm back. They'll notice if I disappear again."

Ryan rushed toward her again and Eden caught him by his arms before he could grab her by her throat again.

"Of course," she said, "that would mean that you would have to kill me, and that isn't going to happen. Not here. Not ever." She shoved against him as he pushed back against her so that they were locked in the battle for dominance. "I won't let you."

"How are you going to stop me?" Ryan asked. "You couldn't hold your own while you were here, and you won't be able to now."

He pushed her and Eden felt herself stumble. She stepped back to catch herself and her foot landed on one of the papers on the floor, causing her to slip and fall onto the table. Ryan was on her immediately. His body draped over her back, pressing her so hard into the edge of the table that pain shot down her legs. Ryan's hand came to the front of her throat and he wrenched her head back.

"There were a lot of fresh young girls who would have loved to be in your position," he hissed. "I chose you because you were a hot piece of ass to look at, but you also knew what the hell you were talking about. I thought it would be fun to get to mix a little business with pleasure."

"You're delusional," Eden said. "No one would want to work with you, and there were certainly no young girls who would have any more interest in you groping them and making indecent proposals every day than I did."

Ryan pulled her head back harder and Eden felt herself starting to choke.

"You never would cooperate with me. You were much too full of yourself and just couldn't be bothered to just go along with me. The thing is, you never seemed to get it through your head that you weren't going to get anywhere in this career without me. Say what you will about me, but I have a respect and a standing in the scientific community that you could never even hope to achieve."

"You only have that because of your family."

Ryan whipped her around and pressed his body to hers again so that she was forced to bend back away from him. Taking her shoes off in the hallway had brought her down so that Ryan towered over her. She knew that there would have been a time that that would have been intimidating, but she had become so accustomed to Pyra and the other Denynso men that it didn't even faze her.

"My family hasn't achieved anything of note in decades. That's my job," Ryan continued. "I'm the one who is going to make the discoveries that are going to change the world."

"You mean that you are going to be the one who will steal the discoveries that are going to change the world," Eden said.

The pressure of Ryan's body on hers was cutting off her air and she was starting to feel dizzy.

"You have no idea what you are talking about," Ryan said, the low, gravely quality of his voice making the words terrifying. "You have no idea what I've accomplished and what I'm going to accomplish. All you know is about the little experiments that we were doing here when you left and this pathetic research."

"Pathetic research?" Eden said, gathering the strength to pull her hands up and press them to Ryan's chest, forcing him back. "It is my 'pathetic' research that started everything that you have supposedly accomplished in the time that I was here."

She gathered the strength that the Denynso blood coursing through her veins gave her and Ryan looked at her with fury and shock in his eyes.

"You don't know anything about the research that I've been doing," Ryan said. Suddenly his eyes sparkled with what Eden could only describe as a dark and vicious laugh. "Maybe I could show you a little of it. Now that you have spent some time with those creatures, it might interest you."

Those words sent Eden over the edge and she forced all of her strength against Ryan in a push that made him stumble away from her. She straightened and glared down at him, her breaths coming out of her in rough, ragged gasps.

"Those *creatures*," she said, "are my clan."

"What do you mean by that?" Ryan asked.

"She means that she is one of us."

Pyra's voice broke through the heated tension in the room and Eden stepped back as her mate lunged at Ryan, tackling him to the ground and pinning him there. His tremendous body dwarfed Ryan and the smaller man had an expression of pure terror on his face.

"What?" Ryan gasped, his hands coming up to grip Pyra's forearms on either side of him.

Eden knew that Ryan had absolutely no chance of overpowering Pyra. The Denynso warrior was not just taller and broader that the human man. He also had the intense, indescribable strength of the warrior kind. When combined with protectiveness for his mate, this strength was something that would be insurmountable for any human.

"She is Denynso," Pyra growled at Ryan, forcing him harder into the ground until Ryan choked with the lack of breath getting into his lungs. "She is also my mate and the mother of my son."

8

———

"Pyra, get off of him," Eden said.

"No," Pyra said back.

Every bit of anger and animosity that he had ever felt toward this man was pouring out of him as he held Ryan to the ground and pressed the palm of his hand to Ryan's throat. He remembered everything that Eden had told him about the way that Ryan had treated her when she worked with him on Earth before she had ever left on her journey to Uoria, and the fears that she had relayed to him before they left on this trip back. He had held that anger inside of him before, unable to do anything about it and knowing that in those moments Eden needed his strength and love more than she needed to see the aggression that burned within him each time that he thought about Ryan. Now, however, the man was lying on the ground beneath him and he had seen for himself what he was capable of when it came to Eden. He had seen the look in Ryan's eyes and heard the sickening blend of hatred and unrequited desire in his voice when he spoke to her.

"Pyra, stop," Eden said again. "You are going to kill him."

"Maybe I want to."

"Pyra, that's not how things work here. You can't just kill on Earth. Especially not like this. You are not at war," Eden told him. "You are in a laboratory and he is unarmed. If you kill him, the government will come after you."

"What can they do?" Pyra asked dismissively.

"They can take you from me and from Lysander."

Pyra's grip on Ryan eased slightly at those words.

"What do you mean?"

"There is no treaty between Uoria and Earth," Eden said. "That is part of what the exchange programs are working toward. If you commit a crime here, you will be taken and put into one of the prisons or in a prison camp. Things work differently here, Pyra."

Pyra's mind wandered to the now-destroyed prison on the edge of the Denynso compound on Uoria. He thought of the cold hallways and dirty, stained cells that they had explored. He thought of Leia and Eliana and what they had told him about their time within the fearsome stone walls of that building. Those images, however, didn't frighten him enough to take away his desire to simply snuff out the life of the man who had made his mate's life so miserable. Instead, it was the thought of being without her and without their son that forced him to release Ryan and stand up.

"I will let you live now," Pyra said down to Ryan, who had made no move to get up from the floor, "but you are never to get near my mate or our child. You have no claim on her life and she will be returning to Uoria with us when we leave. I don't want to see your face again."

Pyra stepped back from Ryan and felt Eden's hands come to his waist. She guided him back further into the laboratory toward the door, but he wouldn't take his eyes off of Ryan until they had backed out of the room and into the hallway. Part of him expected Ryan to get back up and come after them again, but the look of fear on the other man's face told him that he had taken Pyra's words to heart and was going to let them leave without any further resistance.

THEY WALKED out of the building quickly and Pyra remained silent until they had gotten outside again. When the door to the laboratory slammed behind them, he turned to Eden and scooped her into his arms. He buried his face in her hair and held her close to his chest. Soon he felt the heat of her tears soaking through his shirt and her body beginning to tremble.

"Shhhh," he murmured, trying to soothe her. "It's alright now. I'm here. I've got you. He can't get to you now."

She clung to him for several more long seconds and then pulled her face back to look at him.

"How did you find me?" she asked through the tears that were still falling down her cheeks and over her lips.

"I came to look for you at the party and Zuri told me that you said there was something that you had to take care of. I knew that you weren't going after Lysander because if you were you would have come to tell me and we would have gone together. The only other thing that I could think of was that you were coming here to see Ryan."

"You say that like you think that I wanted to see him," Eden said.

"No," Pyra said, shaking his head, "I didn't mean it like that. I know that you didn't want to see him. But there was something that led you here. I will always come find you when you need me."

He eased Eden down to her feet and she brushed the

hair out of her face, trying to regain her composure. She shook her head, took a deep breath, and he saw her eyes flicker back to the door to the building. He reached for her hand and led her away from the door toward the sidewalk.

"Why did you come here?" he asked.

He didn't want his voice to sound angry and potentially upset her any further than she already was. The truth was that he was angry. After all of the anger and fear that she had expressed to him about his man she had still just gone to the laboratory to face him completely alone. Even with the strength that she had gotten from becoming Denynso after her first vicious encounter with the Klimnu, Pyra worried that if he hadn't gotten there when he had, she would have been in very serious danger. Her strength was one thing, but it didn't make her completely invulnerable to other attacks. Had Ryan decided to pick up any kind of weapon, she could have been killed without Pyra ever knowing what was happening.

"He lied about the entire mission that he sent me on," Eden said as they walked toward the public transportation stop.

"What do you mean he lied?"

Pyra felt discomfort roll through his stomach as the sound of the sleek vehicle told him that it was approaching. He hated the strange and uncomfortable mode of transportation, but it had been the only way that he was able to get to Eden in the middle of the party. Zuri had explained to him how to use it, but it had been an unpleasant situation from the moment that he stepped inside. All of the other passengers looked at him with a combination of fear and morbid curiosity as he tried to take his seat in the cramped space. He had been unsure of where he was supposed to get out and had had to explain to the driver where he needed to go. Though he had ended up where he needed to be, the entire ride he had felt like the driver was doing his best to ignore him.

Eden waited as the door to the vehicle opened and she stepped inside. The driver's eyes went from her to Pyra and then back to her as if he was evaluating whether Eden was in danger. A sudden surge of defensiveness washed through him and Pyra reached up to rest his hand on Eden's shoulder. She immediately turned her head and touched a kiss to his hand, which seemed to at once assuage and unnerve the driver.

When they had finally settled into their seats, she turned to him and lowered her voice.

"I thought that there was a formal research trip planned and that Ryan had coordinated with the university and some of the department members who he had already worked with on other projects. Even though this was a new project and the aim that he had for me was completely unethical, as you know, I figured that he had at least found someone else from the university to back him up and get him the necessary clearance to use the university shuttles and connect with Creia in an official capacity."

"That's what we were told," Pyra said.

He still remembered when Eden arrived and Creia assigned him the role of being her guardian and protector. The king had told them that she was a scientist coming to the planet to research Uoria's plants, animal life, and other features. Though he hadn't actually told them that she was a part of the innovative exchange program that he had devised with Earth, it had been the assumption of all of the warriors. They had been receiving researchers and journalists for some time, but most of them arrived with little fanfare and soon left. This woman was highly anticipated, which was why it was even more of a surprise when she arrived and he discovered that she was his intended mate.

Eden shook her head and leaned closer to him.

"It was all a set up," she said. "Which makes it even more conniving because he told me that even though the trip itself was official, my mission to get the blood of the most powerful of the Denynso warriors was a secret. It was a set up within a set up."

Pyra felt his stomach tighten painfully at the words that Eden didn't even seem to realize that she had said.

"You were after my blood?" he asked, continuing to force his voice to remain calm.

Eden looked up into his eyes sharply, her mouth falling open slightly. Though he had known since the moment that she arrived that her underhanded mission on Uoria was to retrieve Denynso blood and bring it back to her boss, she had never told him that he had been specifically named as the warrior whose blood it was she was meant to take. It felt uncomfortably close to a betrayal even though he knew that she hadn't known him when she made the agreement and that she had never made any efforts to hurt him in any way.

"I'm sorry, Pyra," she said. "I didn't know you. I didn't even know that it was going to be you who Creia assigned to watch over me when I got to Uoria. All I knew was what Ryan told me about you."

"What did he tell you?"

"That you were mean and violent. That you would kill anything that crossed your path without a second thought and that you would bed any woman who came close to you and then toss her aside without even bothering to learn her name much less worry about what she was feeling. He told me that your blood was the most powerful substance in the universe, that it could make weapons that no one could defend themselves against."

"And you wanted to be a part of making that kind of weapon?" he asked.

The thought that she was willing to be a part of a project that vicious was completely against everything that he knew about Eden. She was a bit rough around the edges, especially after he met her, and he wouldn't say that she was the gentlest or even the most compassionate of women he had encountered. She was not cruel or uncaring, however, and he found it very hard to believe that she would have been complacent to something as horrific as not only stealing the blood of another creature, but then using that blood to create weapons to destroy as many other living beings as possible.

Eden hung her head and Pyra saw tears dripping onto her lap.

"No," she whispered. "Of course I didn't. Why do you think that I confessed to Creia and Theia as soon as I met them?"

"Because you lost your nerve when you saw me and you knew that if you tried it and they found out what you were doing that they could execute you?"

She looked up at him and the expression in her eyes cut into him.

"Do you really think that, Pyra?" she asked.

"I don't know what else to think."

"I confessed because I didn't want to be a part of it. I wasn't afraid. I could have gotten away with it if I tried, but I didn't want to be a part of it."

"Then why did you come in the first place?"

"I've already told you," she said, the familiar anger starting to build in her voice. "Ryan threatened me. I had already rejected his advances more times than I can count and then I started working on research that he knew was more complex than what he was doing and he wanted it for himself. I had no choice. If I didn't agree to go, I was throwing away my career. He was going to go to the head of the lab and tell them that I was the one who was harassing him, and that I had stolen his research. It would have destroyed my professional reputation and kept me out of any position for the rest of my life."

Pyra knew that the situation was escalating and that he needed to bring it back under control. He reached out and touched her face gently.

"I'm sorry," he said. "I know that you told me all of that. It just hurts to know that you came to Uoria with the intention of stealing my blood."

"I didn't know you, Pyra."

"I know that," he said, "but you were intended for me from the moment that you were born, so it still feels like a betrayal."

"But if I hadn't been sent to Uoria to steal your blood, then I never would have met you. We never would have had a reason to come together."

Pyra realized that she was right. If she had not been sent for that particular mission, they never would have met. She would not have ever come to Uoria, and he would never have had a reason to travel to Earth. He would have spent his entire life aching for the woman who was meant to be his mate and never would have found her.

The vehicle pulled to a stop and Pyra and Eden climbed

off. When it zipped away into the darkness, he reached for her wrist and turned her around so that he could wrap his arms around her waist and look down into her face.

"No matter why it happened, I am happier than I could ever tell you that you came to Uoria when you did."

"I am, too," she said.

Eden's voice still sounded strained.

"Why did Ryan set you up?" he asked.

"He wanted to steal my research. That's why the women were so surprised to see me. He didn't tell them that I was going to Uoria. Even though he told me that he knew that I was sneaky enough to pull off getting the blood that he wanted, he was positive that I was going to mess up and be killed. He told all of the women that I had been devastated by his rejection and moved to a developing planet. That way he could take all of the research that I had already done and all of the notes that I had already made, and didn't have to worry about me coming back and telling anyone what happened. He knew that if I was killed on Uoria, though, that the university would cause serious problems for the planet and everything would come out anyway. So he faked the entire thing. He rented a ship and hired a crew that I would think belonged to the university. That way there would be no questions when I didn't come back."

"Is everything alright?"

Pyra looked up to see Zuri running across the street toward them. She hugged Eden and looked at Pyra as if for explanation.

"Everything's fine," Eden told her. "Pyra just came to get me, but everything is going to be perfectly fine."

Though Eden's voice sounded stronger now, Pyra wasn't convinced. What Ryan had done, and his violent reaction to seeing Eden, was far too complex just to cover up some stolen work. Something more was going on, but he wasn't sure yet what it was. He knew that he would have to be on guard to protect Eden and Lysander, without upsetting her or letting any of the others know his concerns until there was something more that could be done.

9

———

"**I** don't understand why you are doing this," Theia said as Creia crossed the room to a tall bureau and removed several tunics to tuck into his satchel along with the pants that he had already packed inside.

"Because I have to," he said.

"Why?" she asked.

Creia turned to his mate and saw the look of worry and fear in her eyes. He hated that she was feeling that way, and even more that it was him that was causing it, but this was something that he knew that he had to do and he couldn't let her stop him.

"I have to find out more about what happened," he told her. "I have to do more to understand the original Denynso and what happened to them after the clan split and my half came here."

"But why, Creia?" she asked, her voice more imploring as he reached into the drawer at the bottom of another large piece of furniture and pulled out the dagger that he had not touched in many years. "Everything is going so well now. We have already found out so much and everyone is trying to make sense of it all together. The others are coming back from the settlement and soon we'll be able to rebuild all of the relationships that our kind used to have with the others of the planet. Isn't that enough? Can't you just let it go?"

"Let it go?" Creia asked, stunned that his mate would make such a suggestion. "Don't you think that letting it go for so long has caused enough trouble as it is?"

"What do you mean?"

"You see all of the species coming together and making amends. I see the shattering of those bonds that happened to begin with. Something more happened that we don't understand yet, and it is the cause of the turmoil that tore Uoria apart. This compound didn't used to be the only one of the Denynso on the planet. You know that."

"Yes, I do," Theia said, sounding slightly sad as she was forced to remember the difficulty that came when the clan split so many years before.

"So what happened to the others? Why has there been absolutely nothing from them in decades? How did we not know about Loralia's kind right beneath our feet? Why did the Klimnu decide to leave Uoria for Ynn in the first place? If they were so determined to take over the planet, what happened to change their mind?"

"I don't know," Theia admitted, looking taken aback by the sudden stream of questions that he had asked her. "But what good will it do for you to go out there in search of all of these answers? What do you think that you will find?"

"Exactly that," Creia said, putting a few final items into his bag and lifting it over his shoulder. "Answers."

"Will that help anything?" Theia asked.

"There's no way to know that until we find them," Creia said. "We didn't know what the men were going to find out when they left the compound and found the human settlement, or that they would discover the Mikana settlement and make the connection between them and the Klimnu. What I find in the badlands could completely change everything that we know about our own kind, and about the other species on Uoria. I have already let my people down so much. I owe it to them not to keep them in the dark any longer."

"What am I supposed to do while you're gone?" Theia asked.

"You are to lead," Creia said, stroking the side of her face, "just like you always have. You are not alone. You have the few who remained here, and the ones who went to the settlement to release the Mikana should be back soon. If they arrive back before I do, reassure them that I will return and allow them to make themselves at home in the compound. Let them move into the homes that we had set aside for the university program. You are completely safe, my love. The compound is secure just as it always has been."

He leaned forward and kissed his mate deeply, allowing himself just a moment to indulge in the feeling of her so that he could memorize it even more completely than it already was and carry it with him during his travels. Though he had reassured Theia that she was safe in the compound while he was gone, he didn't feel as sure about his own safety. The reality was that he didn't know what was waiting for him in the badlands. He hadn't been on that side of the ridge since he was a very young child, and from what he saw when he brought the others up to look at it just weeks before, it had undergone a brutal and devastating change. The damage that the Valdicians and their allies had done to the land was excruciating, and Creia wondered what other secrets could be hiding down in the smoldering remnants just waiting for him to discover them.

"I will be back," he reassured her. "Everything is going to be just fine."

He kissed Theia again and then walked away, keeping his back to her as he moved toward the back corner of the compound even though he wanted more than anything to turn around and get one more glimpse at her. Part of him knew that if he did, he would run back to her and stay in the palace, allowing his mind to remain cloaked in darkness. He couldn't allow that to happen. He wouldn't fail his people again, no matter what he had to do to make sure that they knew the truth.

CREIA FELT like the way to the ridge was far longer than it had been the last time that he had been up there. It was as if every step that he took extended the distance and it was nearly mid-afternoon by the time that he climbed the last bit of the loose, steep path to stand on the plateau overlooking the badlands. Out of the corner of his eye he saw the small cave where Eden had given birth and he took a moment to feel the happiness that came from that space. It was right here on this ridge where he had become a grandfather. It had also been here that they had learned of the compassion and care that were still so evident in the Mikana as Rey stepped forward to help Eden through the delivery of her tiny son even though he had mere moments before been at the mercy of Pyra. And it was here where Pyra had confessed that he had been overcome by the power that he had in the settlement and by his own fear of the Klimnu and that it had led him to mistreat those who he had been entrusted to lead, and those who he had gone to for help. So much had occurred right in this spot, but Creia couldn't help but also think of all that had happened here long before those moments had even begun.

This was the very ridge that half of the Denynso clan that had inhabited the space that was now the badlands had crossed when leaving that compound behind to begin a new one. This was where Creia had followed his family, clawing their way up the much rougher terrain of the other side in hopes of finding peace and comfort in the more fertile and beautiful land beyond the boundary of the ridge. When he closed his eyes he could still feel the grit in his mouth and the digging of the rocks in his hands as he had clawed. When he opened them it was as though he could see the lingering images of the two times superimposed over each other, still happening, still repeating in the dark orange glow of the afternoon sunlight.

Not all of them had made it to the other side, and he remembered the feeling of watching those who had died slowing, become weaker, and finally no longer moving when they hit the dirt. He didn't realize then that there was more to their deaths than just the journey. Though arduous, the trip had not been so difficult as to kill these strong and powerful men. Instead, something far more ominous had gotten to them. This was part of what had brought him back here so many years later. He needed to know what had happened to them. He wanted to know what had driven that half of the clan away from the others and why they had been kept safe when the others were destroyed.

After resting for a few more minutes on the plateau, Creia gathered his belongings and started the more challenging way down the other side of the ridge. Where there was a path on the other side, the face closest to the badlands was predominantly rough stone and jagged edges. When he was a child he had ridden part of this way on his father's back and the rest of the way he had climbed with his brother's hand supporting him from beneath, helping to lift him up each section so that he wouldn't tumble down again. In those moments as he climbed, he never once imagined that he would be going down the other way one day. His parents had told him that this move was important, something that would change their lives completely and that he was never to look back. They never wanted him to think of the original compound or the others again, and he, along with all of the other young ones and everyone who came after them, had been strictly instructed to stay away from the ridge. That is when the rocks had become a boundary for the compound. They were not to go past the foot of the path, and even then they had to get special permission to even proceed that far.

To ensure that the Denynso who had taken up residence in the new compound didn't stray far from the center of the new land, the king of the time also established boundaries on the other sides so that every member of the clan would know where they were expected to go. It was he who decided that there needed to be a wall along the furthest boundary, and designed that wall to be made of stones taken from the base of the ridge so that everyone who saw them would remember the ridge and the prohibition of going beyond it. Even though he was king now, Creia felt a strange sense of nervousness in his belly as he made his way down the first layer of rocks. Being contained within the compound had become such a reality of life, so much a part of being in the clan, that it had become engrained in their existence. Though he could now acknowledge that it had been merely a measure of control by the reigning king at the time, a way for him to restrict and manage the movements and abilities of the Denynso he ruled, Creia had grown to appreciate the feeling of separation that it created and continued the restrictions when he stepped into the role of being king of the compound.

He knew that things were changing, however, and that soon it was likely the times of the boundaries would be over and the members of the clan would have greater freedom to move about the planet as they pleased. It was a tremendous deviation, but one that Creia knew needed to happen. This was his first step, his first moment of rebellion against the fierce regulation of his youth and the systematic secretiveness and omission that had created the widespread distrust, hatred, and breaking down of bonds throughout the planet.

NIGHT HAD FALLEN by the time that Creia had made his way to the bottom of the ridge and was standing at the edge of the badlands. The air around him was glowing with the flames and ash still pouring from the ground, and for a moment he was mesmerized by the heat and the dancing of the powdery debris in the light. Creia walked carefully around the edge of the fiery expanse close to the foot of the ridge. He dug into his memory, searching for anything that would tell him which direction that he should go. He wanted to find whatever may be left of the original compound and the buildings that had been a part of it, but much like the desire to return, he had blocked much of his memory of the compound out of his mind. He struggled to remember what it had looked like before they had left and before the Valdicians destroyed it so fully and completely. He looked into the distance, following the pattern of the flames, and realized that there were areas that were not engulfed in the fire.

Creia lowered his bag to the ground and reached inside for one of his tunics. He folded the fabric carefully and then wrapped it around his face so that it covered his nose and mouth and tied behind his head. Strapping the bag higher on his back so that it wouldn't catch fire if he slept too close to the flames, he held the fabric to his face and started further into the space. Though he walked on ground that was black rather than glowing red, he could still feel the residual heat coming up through the soles of his feet and tingling on his skin. Creia told himself that he would become accustomed to the heat and pressed forward, looking around himself for any sign of the compound or the Denynso who used to live there.

He had been roaming the space for a few moments when he realized that there were outlines in the blackened ground. They were faint and he had to focus intently into the darkness in order to see them, but he knew that he was seeing what were once the foundations of the Denynso houses that had once filled this area. As he let himself feel the grief and sadness that filled him at that sight of the foundations, the tangible representations of the lives that had once been centered on this compound, Creia also began to feel the exhaustion of his journey pressing down on him. He knew that he needed to sleep or he would never be able to get through another day of his mission.

Creia made his way across the open space, walking around the fires with as far a sweep as he could to avoid the intense heat. Finally he reached the far side and was able to walk away from the strongest of the fires and onto ground that was far cooler. This side of the original compound also had a tall ridge and Creia knew that in the daylight he would be able to see the natural entryway to the compound that was created by the gap between the two ridges as they came toward one another. He moved toward the foot of the ridge and saw a darker outline that indicated a cave. His feet felt heavy as he walked toward the cave and with each step it was as if the bags that he carried dragged on him more intensely. Finally he made it into the cave and stepped far enough in that he no longer felt the searing heat of the flames. The cooler air was soothing and somehow at once made him more tired and more alert. He felt that he wanted to lie down and sleep for hours, but at the same moment his mind was continuing to churn and he wanted to delve deeper, go farther, explore more so that he could feel closer to the answers that he was so desperately seeking. Finally the need for sleep won over and he spread out his blanket roll, laid down, and allowed himself to drift away.

CREIA DIDN'T KNOW how long he slept, but when he opened his eyes the sky outside the cave was still the dark blue of the hour just before dawn. Despite the early hour he knew that he couldn't keep sleeping. He got up, rolled his blanket away, and ate some of the food that Theia had prepared for him. As he was finishing the sun started to come up, filling the space at the front of the cave with its glow. Out of the corner of his eyes he noticed something sparkling in the wall. Creia turned his attention toward it and saw what looked like pieces of shattered glass embedded in the stone.

He ran his fingers along the glass shards and immediately realized that they were not a natural part of the ridge. They had been placed there. Creia looked more closely at the glass and at the wall surrounding the shards. Pale markings in the stone seemed to note what those pieces of glass were and what they meant, but Creia didn't understand them. He pulled a sheath of paper and a pencil from his bag and did his best to copy them, hoping that somehow he would understand them later. He was beginning to turn away to head back out of the cave when he noticed that the cave went deeper than he had originally thought. He took a few steps further, his hand running across the embedded glass in the wall. The further that he walked into the cave, the sharper the pieces of glass became until he felt them biting into his fingers as he walked.

The cave fed into a tunnel and as Creia walked the space grew darker and darker until he wasn't able to see anything ahead of him. He pulled his light stick out of his bag and illuminated it, filling the tunnel with a bright, leading glow. He didn't know where the tunnel led, and no matter how hard he searched the recesses of his memory he couldn't recall this cave or the tunnel from when he was a child living in that compound. He knew that it must have been there. It was not simply created out of nothing, but he felt that he had never seen it before, and certainly had never walked down it. He wondered if this was part of the compound where he hadn't been permitted to go when he was younger, somewhere where the elders of the clan restricted the movements of the others for reasons that stayed shrouded in mystery even among many of the adults.

The further he moved down the tunnel the more that Creia thought of the tunnel that led from the ridge of his compound down to the mirrored realm beneath. It had been that tunnel that had revealed that realm, the place just beneath the compound itself, where Loralia's kind had lived and died, leaving her the only one left of her species. She had lived there for many years completely alone and undetected even by the Denynso who lived just above her. It wasn't until the Klimnu invaded that she saw another creature, and soon she was inundated with others, including Denynso who streamed in to fight what they thought would be the final battle with the gruesome creatures. It bothered him still that every day of his life that he had lived on that compound he had been living above those people, going about his days mere feet above a deep cavern designed as a reflection of the compound above. They had loved that land dearly in the time that they had spent there, but were driven underground by the attacks of other species and a plague that threatened their existence, the same plague that would eventually kill all but Loralia.

The tunnel that had led down to that realm had been hidden away in a ridge just as this one was, but none of the Denynso were small enough to get all of the way down it. Instead they had had to rely on the human women to follow it down until it led them onto the reflected branches of the realm below. Creia felt the ground beneath his feet change and in that instant he realized that just like with the tunnel that led down to where Loralia lived, there was a transporter in this tunnel and he was now much farther away from the cave than the distance that he had walked would entail. The thought made the breath catch in his throat and he lifted he focused ahead of him to the sunlight that he could see faintly in the distance. He walked a little further and the light became bright enough that he was able to put his light stick away and follow the rest of the tunnel by the sunlight alone. After a few more moments he crossed through another cave and out of the mouth into what looked like an abandoned village.

Creia walked out of the cave and across an open space in front of another ridge that was strikingly similar to the ones that bordered his compound and the badlands. He stepped out into the center of the village and looked around, trying to gain his bearings. He had never been to this area of the planet and it was nothing like what the warriors had described when they told him about their mission out of the compound and across the planet. That meant that he had traveled further than they had in a matter of steps, obviously utilizing the same technology that had been put into place in the tunnel that led down to the mirrored realm. He thought back to when they realized that the technology existed in that tunnel and how they immediately assumed that it had been put into place by the human flight attendant and the traitor Denynso who had been aiding the Klimnu in their battles. Now that he realized it also existed in the tunnel that he had just left, Creia wondered if that assumption had been accurate.

He moved further into the village and stepped up to the closest building. The door hung off its hinges, dust coming from inside as though the years were taking over and were gradually washing the village away. Creia carefully moved the door aside and stepped into the building. It was cold and familiar. Low furniture filled the space and began to populate his mind with memories from his childhood. He knew that it wasn't this space that he was remembering, but something very similar, something that looked almost identical. He continued through the small house, touching the forgotten surfaces and letting his eyes travel across personal objects left strewn around as though still waiting for their owners to return and complete the moments that they had been living when those objects had been dropped or placed aside.

The memories continued to come to him as he entered a small room to the back of the house and saw that it was a bedroom. A thick blanket was folded back and there was still a wrinkle in the sheet indicating where the inhabitant slept. Where could that person have gone? Did he know when he climbed out of bed that final morning that he wouldn't be getting back into it that night?

Creia saw a book resting on the table beside the bed and reached for it. The pages were thin and frail, filled with jagged writing. His heart began to pound as he read the words. They were written in a language that he hadn't heard in many years, a language that formed his memories of his mother's voice and whispered the bedtime stories that his grandfather had told him before he fell asleep at night. It was a language that was spoken long ago, before the assimilation that faded the demarcations between the species throughout the galaxy and brought uniformity to spoken and written words. The book was written in ancient Denynso.

Creia flipped through the pages of the journal, forcing his mind to link the sounds and the words until their meanings flooded back to him through the years that had separated them. He could understand them again, read through them with the same speed and comprehension that he had when he was young and that he used now to read the core language. The words spoke of a different time, a time long ago before he was even alive. Creia knew now that he was in a Denynso home from long before his lifetime, before even his parents. The home looked like the home that his grandparents had lived in when he was just a child, reminding him of the afternoons that he had spent there watching his grandmother bake for the clan much the way that Ty did now.

The realization sank into him as he read through the journal that chronicled a life that had been so normal and then had taken a stark and terrifying turn. The words became more irregular and rough on the page as the date on the top of each progressed. He read of an enemy, a darkness that had overtaken the planet, and the ties between the Denynso compounds that were being threatened. Creia had never known about the cooperation between the clans, or the connections that had once existed between the compounds. This compound had ceased many years before he was born, long before the clan had split and formed the new compound, yet he had never even known that they had existed.

What could have happened to them? Where did the clan that had called this compound home go, and what did it have to do with the fear and concern that filled the words on the journal pages?

He knew then that the technology that had existed in the tunnel that brought them down into the mirrored realm had not been the work of the human flight attendant, at least not the original work. It had existed more than a century before in the tunnel that had brought him from the badlands here, which meant it had once been used to allow the Denynso to move from compound to compound quickly and undetected.

A sound in the front of the building made Creia pause. He carefully tucked the journal into his bag and turned to walk toward the door to the bedroom. Before he could take a step, however, a dark figure descended on him and the world around him went black before he hit the floor.

10

"What more do you have to tell us?" Maxim asked.

Ivy cringed at the straightforward bluntness in her mate's voice, but she understood the emotion behind it. Maxim was tired and worn, brought down by everything that was happening around him and the perception that he had nothing that he could do about it. She knew how desperately he wanted to unravel all of the tangled, confusing situations that were building around them, and truly understand once and for all what had happened to his father and what that had to do with everything that had unfolded on Uoria since. Fighting so hard against everything that stood in his way and forcing himself to confront the fact that he didn't know as much about his childhood, his family, and even his species as he thought, however, was draining everything that was inside of him.

The man who she loved was as beautiful inside as he was out, and the gentleness of his heart was making it difficult for him to pick up the burden that he felt Aegeus had left behind and finally bring it to resolution. As challenging as it was for him, however, Ivy knew that he was never going to give up. No matter what he had to face or the pain that he had to put himself through, Maxim was going to do everything that he had to do to find out what had happened and ensure that his home, his planet, and his kind were protected.

Athan stepped back from the doorway and gestured for the three of them to enter. Kyven had gone to Emerie in the home that she was sharing with some of the other women and told her that he would see her later that night. Ivy had watched as the woman's face changed from confused to worried, to saddened. She could almost feel the emotions that were pouring off of her and she ached for the past that Emerie was still struggling to overcome. Though Ivy didn't know Emerie well and didn't know who she was in the years before she left Earth as part of Nyx 23, she did know that there was something the woman was carrying that she hadn't yet come to terms with, and wasn't yet ready to reveal to Kyven. It was hurting her deeply, but she was fighting to push its influence away even as she eased into the relationship that was gradually building between the two of them.

When they had settled into the main room once again Athan took a moment to look at each of them in the eyes carefully.

"Are you sure that you want to know?" he asked, pausing with his eyes locked on Maxim's. "Are you sure that you are prepared to hear what I have to say this time?"

His tone was slightly scolding and Ivy felt herself tense. She worried that Athan would set Maxim off again and she didn't know if she had the energy to cope with the emotions that seeing her mate go through these sudden and intense swings caused in her. She wanted to be there for him, to offer him the support, encouragement, and help that she had promised when they first discussed not going back to Earth but instead heading back to the settlement to free the other Mikana from the meeting hall where Pyra had secured them. As they were sitting there, however, and she realized just how deep this situation was spinning, she felt like she wasn't able to live up to that aspiration and was in a way letting Maxim down. All she could do was sit beside him, hold his hand, and hope that somehow her presence was enough.

"I'm ready," Maxim said.

The vitriol was gone from his voice and his tone seemed to satisfy Athan. The older man glanced at Kyven.

"I take it your brother has told you what I told him?"

"Yes," Kyven responded.

"I told you that your father found out about the Klimnu influencing the Order," Athan said. He looked at each of the men for affirmation before moving on. "Aegeus wouldn't tell me the names of the men, but he did say that some of the most powerful of the Order, men who were rarely seen and only by invitation, had transitioned and were now fully Klimnu. The level of secretiveness within the Order is something that I don't think you could ever understand. This organization is meant to be unknown to any who are not within it, but even within the number of the Order there are secrets. Many have never seen the men who are at the highest ranks. I am one of them. When Aegeus told me that he knew that some of these men were now Klimnu and had begun to influence the Order, even those who had not transitioned, he wouldn't tell me the names of the men, only that it was their words that was arranging our movements within the Order, and that they were going to use that tactic to get the rest of the kingdom under the command even further. The final goal was to take over the entire planet with the Klimnu at the helm and the Mikana close behind."

"If Papa knew who these men were, why didn't he just tell someone so that something could be done?" Kyven asked.

Ivy looked at him and saw an expression in his eyes that was almost painfully hopeful, like a little boy who just didn't want to believe that there could be anything wrong with the choices that his heroic father made so many years ago.

"Who was he to tell?" Athan asked. "Remember that even the leader of the kingdom doesn't know about the Order. It was the same then. The Order has long acted as a check of power, a balance in a way. As long as the Order existed, the king would not be able to rule with too extensive of authority or too aggressive of a hand. If Aegeus had mentioned the Klimnu and what they were doing, it would have caused mass hysteria and would have revealed the existence of the Order. That would have put the entire clan at risk. He knew that if something was to be done, he had no choice but to handle it himself."

"You didn't offer to help him?" Maxim asked.

Ivy could hear the familiar softness returning to his voice and she slid closer to him. She couldn't imagine what he was going through.

"Of course I did," Athan said, looking at Maxim and then Kyven with sincerity in his eyes that cut through Ivy and made her chest ache.

As deeply as she felt the pain that her mate was feeling, she also couldn't help but feel compassion for the older man who was sitting in front of her. He looked worn and some-what broken, as if he had been carrying a tremendous burden for years and it was pulling him down even as he struggled to hold himself up.

"What did he tell you?" Ivy asked.

Athan turned to look at her as if he had forgotten that she was there.

"He wouldn't tell me anything," Athan said. "I knew what he had learned about the Klimnu and the members of the Order, but he wouldn't tell me anything about what he planned to do. We already knew that there was going to be a battle and I assumed that he was going to put whatever plan he had into action during that battle, but he wouldn't tell me what it was. It was only moments into the battle when the Valdicians, the Klimnu, and their allies descended on him and he was gone. He never had the opportunity to tell me what he was going to do. If he had, I would have done it for him. I would have done anything to avenge him and ensure that the hopes that he had for the planet were fulfilled."

"What did the others of the Order do when you told them about his death?" Kyven asked.

"Nothing," Athan said. "They told me that it was my responsibility to inform your family, but that that was all that I was to do. I was barred from delving any further into the situation or doing any kind of investigation of my own. I wasn't even permitted to go back to the battlefield to see if there was any way that I would be able to find any sign of him, even his armor. I wanted to have something to bring back to your mother to keep of him since I couldn't bring back his body."

"Why wouldn't they want you to look into it anymore? Didn't they want to know what had happened to him?" Ivy asked.

"I have no explanation for that," Athan said. "When the battle ended and we accounted for the lost, it was only Aegeus whose body couldn't be recovered."

"What happened to the others?" Maxim asked. "How did you explain to those families what had happened to them?"

"The Order had protocol for how to handle these situations. Since they didn't want to discuss the wars with those who weren't in the Order, they had a process for explaining deaths and other problems that would assuage the families without revealing the presence of the Order or the conflicts with the others. It wasn't as difficult as you would think. Aegeus was a bit of an anomaly when it came to the Order. He was the only man who had a wife and children and was still in the Order. It was the same with his father before him. In the past there had been more men who had come into the Order with families or who had started families once they were already in the Order. In more recent years, though, it became tradition for only men who were unmarried and had no families of their own to be a part of it. It made situations like this far easier. It is much less difficult to explain away a grown man going missing when he has no ties than it is to tell a wife and young ones that their husband and father are gone."

"You have never married, have you, Athan?" Ivy asked.

Athan shook his head.

"No. My life was devoted to the Order. I think that is why Aegeus and his family meant so much to me. I knew that I would never have a wife and children of my own, so in a way it was as if I could enjoy the feeling of having a family when I could be with all of them."

"You were a part of our family," Kyven said.

Athan looked to him and Ivy saw Maxim nod.

"You still are," Maxim said. "You meant so much to Papa. I know that he would be proud that you have stayed with the Order and have done what you can to finish what he started."

They were the words that Maxim had used to describe what he meant to do, and Ivy felt their meaning sinking into her as Maxim said them.

"I didn't know that the Mikana married," Ivy said softly.

She knew that it was out of context and didn't really matter to the conversation, but somehow it bothered her. The Denynso knew nothing of marriage and instead had bonds created in truly beautiful but private ways personal just to each couple. It startled her in a way to find out that this species, the species that had borne the man who she loved with every fiber of her being, not only understood but apparently participated in marriage as hers did. She didn't know if it should bother her that Maxim had never mentioned it or if she should simply accept that no matter how deeply she had already invested herself in him that they were still getting to know each other. This may simply be something that she would have learned later.

"It's not quite the same as humans," Athan told her. "The ritual itself is different and from what I learned from those who had the opportunity to interact with the people of the Nyx 23 settlement before it was locked by the Covra, there are some complex legal issues related to marriage on Earth that don't fit in with our kind."

Ivy had never heard marriage described in such harsh terms and she was taken aback by it. She looked to Maxim, who stroked her cheek gently.

"The Mikana and humans are different, my love. This is all something that we will talk about in time."

11

———

"**I**f you could leave the kingdom right now, would you?"

Zyyr stroked his fingers through Lila's hair as he stared up at the purple and green sunset above them. It was that breathtaking time of day when the evening had night quite ended but the night was already beginning, putting him in the strange, somewhat ethereal mood of wanting to make the most of the last gasps of the day while also wanting to let the soft impending darkness of night soothe him to sleep.

Lila sighed beside him and nuzzled closer.

"I don't know," she said softly.

"You said that you wanted to know what was outside," he said, looking down at her.

"I know," she said, her hand running softly across his chest as her leg came up to drape across his. "But what if I got out there and it was dangerous? What if I have had these amazing images of the planet outside of the kingdom but when I got out there, I didn't like it?"

"What if you did?"

Lila took a deep breath.

"I don't think that I'm ever going to have the opportunity to find out. We are meant to stay within the boundary of the kingdom. It's just the way that it is, Zyyr. Dreaming isn't going to change it and sometimes I wonder if it hurts too much to even let myself wonder."

Zyyr felt his heart tighten in his chest. He hated to hear her talk that way. They had been out by the orchard for hours after they had eaten the last of their picnic and in that time he had only become more sure that his mind, heart, and body were telling him that this incredible woman was meant to be his mate. Love that he couldn't explain surged through his veins and he felt himself more drawn to her with each breath. Hearing the sadness and longing in her voice hurt him deeply. He had been telling the truth when he told her that most of the Denynso had never questioned the fact that they didn't leave the compound and were expected to simply live their lives in the place. As Lila had said, it was just the way it was and the warriors had been bound by their sense of duty and loyalty to such an extent that they never thought to wonder what could be beyond the life that their king had created and dictated for them.

Now that they had come out of the compound, however, Zyyr could understand what Lila was feeling. He could no longer imagine not being able to leave and not knowing what else the planet had to offer beyond the small area where he was born. He could hear that sense of tension in her voice now, the pull between loving her home and still wanting to step beyond the walls that stopped her and gain a new perspective.

"What is stopping you, Lila?"

Lila sat up and looked down at him, her eyes searching his.

"The expectations of everyone in the kingdom."

"And if you broke those expectations?" he asked, sitting up and resting his hands on her waist. "What would happen?"

"I don't know," she responded quietly after a short pause.

Zyyr smiled at her and leaned forward to rest his lips to hers. The touch ignited something inside him and he jumped to his feet, taking her by her hands to help her up.

"Let's find out," he said.

Lila's eyes widened and she shook her head slightly.

"What do you mean?" she asked.

"I mean let's find out," he said. "There's nothing to stop you, Lila. There are no laws, no formal restrictions to keep you here. Like you said, it is only expectations, and no one ever got anywhere by always following expectations."

"How would you know?"

Zyyr knew that she didn't mean the words as aggressively as they had sounded, but they sank into him painfully. He took a breath and pulled her a little closer.

"I know because I followed them my entire life and I never did anything that every other warrior of my kind hasn't done. I never saw anything or did anything. I never accomplished anything or experienced a single day that was anything different than the life that my brothers and father lived. When that ended, though, when I finally got to step onto the other side of that wall and do the things that I thought that I would never do, that I didn't even know were available to do, that is when I started to live. I was expected to follow everything that Pyra said when we were in the settlement, and I went against that. Instead, I joined those who stood up against him and helped to ensure that the Mikana stayed as safe as possible. I was expected to go back to the Denynso compound after the Mikana men were freed, but instead I chose to join Maxim, Ivy, and the others coming here. And I met you."

"Does that matter to you?" she asked softly, lowering her eyes and then looking back up at him.

Zyyr felt his heart swell and his stomach clench. He didn't know how much longer he was going to be able to resist her. He was thankful for the quiet time that they got to spend together away from the others, away from any of the Denynso men who may have ignited the fury and violence in him that was one of the hallmarks of the warriors finding their mates. This allowed him to enjoy being close to her rather than focusing on keeping others away until they could complete their bond. He stepped up closer to her and ran his fingers through her hair, letting his fingers graze around the curve of her cheek.

"It matters to me more than I can tell you," he said. "You are something that I never, ever expected, but I want to break these expectations more than I have ever wanted anything." Lila smiled and he could see the willingness and desire in her eyes. "Come on," he said.

Lila allowed him to take her hand and guide her away from their picnic into the orchard.

"Where are we going?" she asked.

"How far have you gone into this orchard?" he asked.

"About halfway, I suppose," she answered. "Why?"

"There has to be more beyond that," he said, "and beyond that is the boundary to the kingdom. We'll go that far, and then we'll see how you feel."

Lila took a breath and nodded. They walked along quietly, each enjoying the cool shade of the trees and the sweet scent that the fruit added to the air. Zyyr could feel the desire coiling in his belly intensifying with each step that they took further into the darkness and isolation of the orchard. Beneath his feet he could see the paths worn by the steps of the Mikana women who came into the trees to gather food, the trails as straight and consistent as the growth patterns of the trees. The further that they moved into the orchard, however, the less defined the paths became and the more wild the trees appeared.

Though they still grew in the even, meticulous lines. The trees further into the orchard seemed to reach into the sky with more abandon and spread branches laden with heavy, vibrant fruit. Lila lifted one of her slim, graceful hands and ran her fingertips along one of the pieces of fruit that hung low enough for her to reach.

"Everything looks so different back here," she said almost as though she were speaking to herself.

"No one ever comes back here," Zyyr said, "so there are no expectations holding the trees back."

He had meant the comment playfully, but Lila looked back at him with a serious look in her wide eyes. She didn't say anything to him, but Zyyr felt as though something had changed within her as they continued forward at a slightly faster pace. They had walked on for several more minutes and the sky above them had shifted from the bright colors of sunset to a velvety blue that somehow seemed to make the space around them feel warmer and more secure. Finally Zyyr looked ahead of him and saw the wall.

Unlike the wall at the front of the kingdom, the stones of this boundary were covered in vines and leaves. His mind immediately returned to the first time that the Denynso warriors had seen the wall of the Nyx 23 settlement. It had looked very much like this one, old and forgotten, left to offer itself up to the planet around it as if the last hands that had touched it had been the ones that had forged it. There, however, the wall had been the same around the entirety of the settlement; at least, as much as Zyyr had seen. Here the wall at the front of the kingdom was clean and well-maintained, beautiful and new even though he knew that it had been built many generations before. It was as if the wall itself was the embodiment of what he was learning about the world around him since he had left the compound. What he saw at first could be lovely and pristine, but he never knew what he would discover if he just delved far enough.

Lila approached the wall and reached out to rest her hand on one of the stones. He expected her to pause there for a few moments, to think about the significance of this moment. Instead, she looked over at him, gathered her skirts, and started to climb. Zyyr closed the space between them and reached out for her, grabbing her by her waist and lifting her up so that she could grab the top of the wall with her arms and pull herself up. When she was sitting securely at the top of the wall, he scrambled up after her.

"There it is," he said to her when he settled into place beside her.

"It is," Lila said back, her eyes trained on the night-cloaked expanse of the planet beyond the wall.

"Do you want to go back?" he asked.

"When you got to the top of the wall of the Denynso compound for the first time, did you want to go back?" she asked.

"No," he answered.

Lila's face turned to him and he saw that she was even more breathtaking in the light of the stars that touched her now that she was out of the cover of all of the trees.

"Neither do I."

Zyyr jumped down and opened his arms to her. She leapt forward, allowing him to catch her and gather her close to his chest for a moment before lowering her to her feet.

"Where do we go now?" she asked.

"Anywhere you want to," Zyyr responded.

The air around them seemed cooler and softer now that they were out of the orchard. He wondered if this moment was as heavy for Lila as his first moment outside of the compound had been for him. It had been a strange feeling, something that he didn't know if he would be able to explain. It was as if he was struggling with himself as he took his first breaths in the openness of Uoria. At once he felt liberated and out of control. The compound had never felt restrictive to him when he was young, it had simply been home. Leaving had never crossed his mind until Pyra began to talk about going out onto the planet to explore and find out what else was out there, so he had never had the opportunity to feel like he was being held back or kept from something. It was exhilarating being beyond the boundary for the first time, but he had also felt somewhat unsure, like he was distancing himself from something that would never be the same. It was almost like a tiny child taking their first steps from their mother. The compound had always kept him safe and protected, and though he knew that what they were doing was important and necessarily for the growth and survival of their kind, he still felt somewhat unsure and as though he would never really be able to feel that sense of blind, trusting protection again.

The grass was high around their legs as they walked, but after a few moments Zyyr felt the ground beneath his feet grow softer and more difficult to traverse. In the light glowing from the sky he was able to see that the grass was giving way to loose sand and in the distance he could hear the whispering of water lapping onto a shoreline.

"What is this?" Lila asked as they got closer to a tremendous body of water stretching from the sandy bank.

Zyyr thought of the water in the Denynso kingdom and the last time that he was there, gathered with the others as they said goodbye to Jem. It was so similar he felt like he could almost see the outline of the women kneeling at the water's edge as the men stood and watched his raft disappear.

"It's a lake," Zyyr told her. "I can't see how big it is right now, but it seems like it goes on pretty far."

As they approached the water the air suddenly felt thick and filled with electricity. The weather was shifting again and Zyyr worried that there was a storm building.

"Maybe we should go back," he said.

"Why?" Lila asked. "We just got out here."

"I know," Zyyr said, "but it feels like there's –"

Before he could get the rest of the sentence out of his mouth there was a massive crack of thunder and it seemed like the sky above them was torn away as a deluge of cold, stinging rain poured down on them. Lila gasped and curled into him. He tried to shield her from the rain, but within moments they were both drenched and he could feel the intense chill of the water seeming to seep into his skin. They ran back to the wall and he clambered up it first, turning around to grab her by her wrists so that he could pull her up and over with him. The branches of the trees provided some cover from the rain, but the drops were still able to get to them and with each step Zyyr felt colder and more dragged down by the heaviness of his wet clothes.

He was heading back toward the houses in the front of the kingdom, but they were nearly out of the orchard when Lila gave his arm a pull and directed him in the opposite direction.

"Where are we going?" he asked.

Another blast of thunder drowned out her answer, but a few moments later he saw a small building hunkered close to the ground several yards away. It didn't look like anybody had gone near it in years, but the door opened smoothly and easily beneath Lila's hand and she was able to reach for a lamp within just a few steps of the door and fill the space with a soft glow.

Zyyr looked around himself, taking in what looked like an old yet carefully preserved and maintained home.

"This was my great-grandmother's house," she told him. "Her father build it for her as a gift for her wedding."

"Why is it so far out here away from all of the rest of the houses?" Zyyr asked.

"She was...," Lila paused as though carefully considering her words so that she could choose exactly what she wanted to say, "different from the others of the kingdom in her time."

"What do you mean?" Zyyr asked.

Lila didn't respond but moved across the house toward a large fireplace. She looked comfortable in the space and he knew that this was not the first time that she had visited the home recently.

"You spend a lot of time here, don't you?" he asked, walking toward the fireplace and watching as she reached into a brushed brass box to pull out tools and start building a fire.

"I'm different from the others of the kingdom, too," she said simply.

12

———

Samira realized that she was gripping the front edge of the backseat of the car so tightly that her hands were cramping and she let go so that she could stretch and rub them, distracting herself from the nervousness that rolled through her belly by trying to bring the feeling back to her fingertips. She looked out of the window to the car and saw a grey, foggy world beyond. It was only the day after her party and yet she felt like the merriment and fun of the celebration was so far distanced from where she was now that it was barely even her own memory. It was more as though she were looking into someone else's memory and trying desperately to live vicariously through it so that she didn't have to really come to terms with what she was doing.

"Are you sure that you want to do this?" Zuri asked her from the driver's seat.

Samira looked up into the rearview mirror and saw her dear friend gazing back at her through the reflection. She tried to look calm and give a confident smile, but all she could muster was a vague nod of her head.

"Yes," she said. "Well," she looked out the window again, "no. I don't want to do this," she admitted, "but it's something that I have to do. I won't be able to go through with the wedding until I have."

She felt Ty's hand slide onto her thigh and give it an affectionate squeeze, and Samira covered his hand with hers to squeeze back. Having him sitting beside her, just knowing that he was there and that she wasn't going to be going through this without him was comforting. It made her feel stronger to know that when she climbed those steps again, so soon after she ran down them and told herself that she never wanted to see the house, much less the man inside it, ever again, she would have Ty by her side to reassure her.

"You know that we are all here for you and that we won't let anything happen to you," Ero said from the passenger seat beside Zuri.

"I do," Samira said.

Zuri smiled at her in the reflection again.

"Well, it's good to hear that you have your line memorized. You just keep practicing that in your mind and this will be over before you know it."

Samira smiled but even as the rest of the car chuckled she couldn't help but let her mind wander back to the last time that she had been in her mother's house and how horribly the situation had unfolded. Zuri and Ero had been there that time as well. They had brought her to the house to help her get a few things so that she could be ready for her journey to Uoria, but instead it had turned into a tense, violent battle between Ero and her stepfather. Though it never would have been an even match even had her stepfather been completely sober, the clash had been awful to watch and she knew that it had taken all of Ero's restraint just to prevent him from destroying his unworthy opponent.

She didn't know if he would be able to exhibit the same level of control this time and could only hope that when they arrived at the house she would be able to spend some time with her mother in peace. Perhaps this would be one of the many evenings that her stepfather spent bellied up to one of his favorite bars and she would be able to escape the situation without even having to see him. If she was truly fortunate, she would never have to see him again.

The car pulled up in front of her mother's house and Samira felt everyone in the car turn to look at her expectantly. She wasn't sure what they thought that she was going to do, and as she looked up at the darkened, quiet house, she didn't really know what to do, either. Part of her wanted to just tell Zuri to drive away, to let her put that house and everyone and everything in it behind her so that she didn't have to think about it anymore and could just focus completely on the new life that was ahead of her. The other part, however, actually did have the compulsion to go through with this. Even though the thought of facing him again made her stomach turn and reminded her of the dark and terrifying nights that she used to spend cowering from him in her bedroom or escaping through her window so that she could hide away in the garage without him being able to find her, she was different now. That part of her wanted him to see her strong and happy, standing by the side of her mate and telling him that he didn't break her and that her life was going to go on just fine without him being a part of it, no matter what he had done to her.

Suddenly the front door to the house opened and a figure darkened the pale blue rectangle of light that indicated the only thing that was on in the house was the ever-present television. Samira felt her muscles tense. She knew not only that silhouette, but its stance. Not only was her stepfather most certainly in the house, but he had already stumbled home from the bar and was now toppling headlong into the rows of beer he kept on the bottom shelf of the refrigerator. This would make him even more impulsive and mean, bringing her back to days that she would much rather forget.

"Who's that?" he shouted into the quickly darkening evening air.

"You're alright," Ty said soothingly, squeezing her thigh again as if in response to the defensive tightening of her muscles. "Everything is going to be fine."

"We're here with you, Samira," Zuri said. "There's nothing that can happen to you now."

Samira took a breath and nodded, then reached for the handle of the car door. As soon as it opened, a flood of anger surged through her. It was an unexpected rush of emotion, a burning intensity that felt like the suppressed feelings and reactions of her lifetime finally releasing inside of her so that she could feel them fully now that she knew that she didn't need to be afraid. She stepped out of the car onto the street and slammed the door, ensuring it was loud enough to startle her stepfather standing at the door.

"Who parked their damn car in front of my house and is disrupting my relaxing time with all of that noise?" he demanded.

Samira came around the back of the car toward the end of the walkway that would lead up to the door and she saw another figure appear in the light of the doorway. It was smaller, though far from slight, and she felt her heart swell a little.

"Samira?" her mother's faint voice said.

"Yes," Samira said, starting up the walkway as fast as she could on her shaking legs.

It was no longer fear or even worry that was making her tremble. Instead it was the surge of adrenaline and anger that was making her muscles twitch and her body shake with the pent-up energy and aggression she was finally allowing herself to feel. Behind her she could hear the footsteps of Zuri, Ero, and Ty coming after her and she felt empowered by their presence. She realized then that it was not that she wanted them there to protect her. Instead she felt strengthened just by the reality of their existence and the new life that she had begun on Uoria. They were proof that she was capable of getting through life on her own and that she was not broken down or destroyed by her stepfather, no matter how hard he had tried. By them being there with her, she was showing him that he didn't own her and that she was not under his command; that she never would be again.

"What are you doing here?" her stepfather demanded, taking one step out of the house so that he leaned against the outside of the doorframe and she could see the beer bottle dangling in his hand.

"I'm here to talk to my mother and get my stuff," Samira answered.

"There's nothing of yours here," he slurred viciously.

"That room is still hers," Valerie said.

"Keep out of my conversation," he said, turning just enough that he could push Samira's mother backwards further into the house.

That single move galvanized Samira and she took off running toward the house. She could hear the others coming up behind her and in moments Ero had overcome her. The warrior surged up the front steps to the porch and dove toward her stepfather, causing him to stumble back and crash onto the floor. The bottle of beer flew from his hand and shattered, sending glass a spray of dark, dank-smelling liquid out onto the porch. In an instant Ty was past Samira and trying to pull Ero up.

"What the hell do you think you're doing?"

"I thought you would have learned the last time that I was here," Ero growled, shoving the man harder onto the floor. "I told you to never put your hands on your step-daughter or your wife again."

Ty finally succeeded in dragging Ero to his feet and Samira helped to push him backwards into Zuri's arms. She knew that it was her time to step forward. This was not the time for her to rely on other people to speak for her. She couldn't settle for just being ushered through the house and then back out to the car. This may be her only opportunity to confront the man who had tormented her and her mother for so long, and to know that she had been the one to look him in the eye and ensure that he knew that her heart, her mind, and her spirit hadn't been lost, even if there were times when she felt like she could no longer reach them.

Samira walked across the room to her mother and crouched down to wrap an arm around her shoulders.

"Are you alright?" she asked.

Valerie looked up into her eyes, staring at her as if not really believing that she was there.

"She's fine."

Samira rubbed her mother's arm comfortingly and stood up, turning calmly to face her stepfather.

"I wasn't speaking to you," she said.

"What did you say?"

"I wasn't speaking to you, Trevor."

The word came from her lips like fire. She hadn't even allowed herself to think of her stepfather's name in so long, much less said it, and now that she had it felt as powerful as a physical blow. He couldn't control her any longer. He didn't have the right or the power to control what she thought, did, or said, and she wouldn't let him think that he did for another moment.

"What did you say to me?"

Samira squared her shoulders toward Trevor and looked him directly in the eyes. For the first time she realized that he was not as much bigger than her as he had always seemed.

"I said that I wasn't speaking to you. I was speaking to my mother. She is a grown woman and she has the ability to speak for herself. She doesn't need you to do it for her."

"Don't tell me what to do in my house, you insolent child."

"This isn't your house," Valerie said. Samira whipped toward her mother, shocked at the sudden sound of strength in her voice. "This isn't your house," she said again, standing and facing off against Trevor, "and she isn't your child. She is my child and this is my house. They were both mine well before you came along."

Samira was startled by her mother's assured stance against Trevor, but also thrilled to hear her finally speaking up for herself after so many years. She hoped that it would be enough to make the man step down, but instead he turned to Samira and took a threatening step forward toward her. Ty stepped forward, but Ero and Zuri took him by his arms and guided him back carefully. The energy in the room was high and tense, but Samira wasn't backing down.

"How dare you come in here with these," he looked back at Ero and Ty and looked them up and down with an expression of disgust on his face, "things and get into my wife's head? We were doing just fine with you gone and now you come back here and get her acting up."

"She's not a child, and they are not things. These are men, and this," she took a step backwards and took Ty's hand so that she could pull him forward beside her, "is Ty. He's my fiancé."

"Your what?" Trevor said with pure vitriol in his voice.

"We are getting married this weekend," Samira said.

She looked over at her mother and saw the sparkle in her eyes. Even beneath all of the pain and anger in the expression, there was excitement and happiness. Samira offered a smile and looked up at Ty.

"We met when she came to my planet with Zuri," Ty said. "She is my mate."

"The Denynso don't marry," Samira explained. "Ty is the first."

"He's willing to do that for you?" Valerie asked.

"I asked her," Ty responded. "I love her and I want to do anything that I can to make her happy. I'm not sure what all of this entails, but I am willing to do anything that she would want me to do so that we can spend our lives happily together."

"What kind of man does whatever a woman would want him to?" Trevor scoffed.

"One who is worth spending your life with," Samira said.

"I'm a real man," Trevor said. "My word is law here and your mother is perfectly happy with me. She knows what's good for her and she stays in her place."

Samira saw Valerie look to Trevor, her eyes wide and frightened, and for a moment she worried that her mother was going to hand herself back over to her husband. She worried that her mother would feel that she had exerted herself enough and that just as she had so many other times before, she would stand up to protect Trevor rather than thinking about what was good for herself.

"No," Valerie finally said. "Not anymore."

"Stop talking, Valerie," Trevor said.

"No," she repeated. "I'm not happy and I haven't been in nearly as long as I've known you. A real man doesn't treat a woman, or a child, the way that you have treated us. Get out."

Samira could see her mother shaking, but she was standing tall, her shoulders as strong and squared as Samira had ever seen them. She stepped up beside her and wrapped her arm around her shoulders to hold her steady, and met Trevor's eyes.

"I believe she told you to do something," she said. "You've given enough commands in your day that I'm sure you know how to follow them."

"I don't have to go anywhere," Trevor said. "I'm your husband and that means I have the right to be here whether it is your name on the deed or not."

There was an arrogant hint in Trevor's voice and Samira felt her fists clench.

"She told you to get out," Samira said.

"Samira," Zuri said. Her voice was calm and even, offering the same soothing effect that it always had. "Unless your mother is going to call the police and file charges against him, she can't force him out of the house. He's lived here with her for long enough that he has the right to be here. The only thing that she can do is evict him, and since he is her husband, that will be difficult."

"See?" Trevor said. "There's nothing you can do about me being here, so you might as well just shut your mouth and get them gone so that I can deal with you."

"You won't be dealing with anybody," Ero said. "Either

you leave now or we will take Valerie with us and see to it that you get a formal escort out of here tomorrow."

"I'll go with you," Valerie said. "It will be nice to spend a night away from this house. I'll go to the judge tomorrow."

Samira felt her heart soar with pride as Valerie stepped away from her and started down the hallway toward her bedroom. Trevor watched after her with a dumbfounded look on his face. For a moment Samira worried that he would go after her, but instead he crossed the living room and dropped down into the worn recliner where he spent the majority of his life. A few minutes later Valerie came back into the room carrying two bulging suitcases.

"Is there anything that we can help you with?" Ty asked.

"There's another suitcase in the bedroom," Valerie said.

Ty headed down the hallway and Valerie turned to Trevor. Samira watched as her mother's eyes scanned the man to whom she had devoted her life for so many years and had been rewarded only with pain and disappointment. She said nothing, but turned away and walked out of the front door, her face directly ahead and her focus not wavering until she climbed into the back of the car.

As soon as the door closed and Samira settled into place beside her mother, she felt Valerie's shoulders drop. It was as if all of the tension that she had held within her since the beginning of her marriage to Trevor had just released and for the first time in all of those years she was able to relax.

"Are you alright?" Samira asked.

"I will be," Valerie said, offering a hint of a smile that would be the first that Samira had seen on her mother's face in as long as she could remember.

"I'm proud of you," Samira said.

"So am I," Zuri offered, glancing back at them in the

rearview mirror. "It couldn't have been easy for you to say that to him."

"It might have taken me a longer time than I would like to admit to finally realize all of what I said to him, but Samira made me see it."

"I did?" Samira asked.

Valerie reached over and took Samira's hand, giving it a squeeze that was as much to reassure her daughter as it was to reassure herself.

"Yes," Valerie said. "I realized that if you were strong enough to not only leave the planet, but to leave and find a man who truly loves you and is willing to change his entire life for you, then I am strong enough to give myself a different life."

13

"Why are you different?" Zyyr asked.

Lila looked back at him from the roaring flames that had built up in the fireplace.

"Take off those wet clothes," she said.

"What?"

He was taken aback by the departure from his question and her sudden, forward request.

"That rain isn't going to be stopping any time soon. There's no reason for you to stay wet, cold, and miserable while you wait. Let me put your clothes by the fire so that they can dry."

She was obviously avoiding his question and he wondered if she had meant to say what she had about her great-grandmother or if it had simply come out. Whatever the reason, she didn't want to continue the thought, and instead was slowly releasing the ties of her dress. She wasn't looking at him as she did it and Zyyr wondered if he should be watching. He tried to divert his eyes, but his intense, nearly overwhelming desire for her kept pulling them back.

The lamp suddenly went out and Lila gasped, turning to look over her shoulder at the darkened lamp.

"I must not have set the solar panel last time I was here," she said. "There wasn't enough energy conserved to keep the lamp going."

"It's alright," Zyyr said. "The fire gives us plenty of light."

Lila nodded and turned her back to him again. The light of the fire framed her, creating her silhouette against the dancing orange and red flames. As he watched her carefully undressing he complied with her request, starting by peeling away his sopping shirt and resting it on the table beside him. They undressed cautiously; apart yet together in their slow, careful revealing of their bodies.

When Lila was completely bare she remained facing the fire, her hands coming up to move through her wet hair, lifting it so that the heat from the flames could work on drying it as it was her skin. Zyyr watched until he couldn't resist her any longer. He walked up behind her and stood close enough that he could just feel the front of his body lightly grazing the back of hers. Lila's hands slowly lowered to her side and she took a breath, synchronizing with his so that the only sound in the room was their shared exhalations.

Finally Zyyr brought his hands to her hips and guided her back a few steps away from the intensity of the heat. When they were further in the darkness of the room he turned her gently in his hands and then let his fingers run down the full swells of her hips until they fell away from her soft, warm skin. He lowered himself to his knees in front of her, the new position bringing his face level with her breasts. He leaned forward to rest his cheek against the front of her ribcage. Her hand settled onto the side of his head as he paused, listening to the rhythm of her heart and enjoying the soft rise and fall of her breaths. After a few moments he turned his head so that he could touch his lips to her skin. It was more a brush of his mouth than truly a kiss, but he could feel her shudder lightly.

He moved his mouth down, resting a slightly more insistent kiss against her belly. He continued his slow, patient progress until he reached the soft valley between her hipbones. The heightened senses that came with knowing that she was his mate meant that he could smell her body responding to his touch and it threatened the control that he was working hard to maintain. Zyyr kissed his way to one of her hip bones and drew the tip of his tongue across it softly. She drew in a breath and Zyyr waited until she calmed to repeat the tender touch on the other hipbone. When finished, he rose higher on his knees again, letting his nose glide up the center of her belly until his face was nestled between her breasts again.

Zyyr took a deep breath and lifted both hands to cup her breasts, slowly filling his palms with her soft flesh and letting his fingers mold around them. Her back arched slightly and he kneaded into her, gently kissing her skin. Lila's hand ran along the back of his head and onto his neck, her fingernails softly dragging along his skin until a shiver ran down his spine. She slowly eased herself onto her knees in front of him and for a moment they were suspended, their breath lingering between them and their hearts beating in time, pounding toward each other.

Gradually, each moving with the caution of the unknown and yet absolute certainty, their faces drew closer to one another. Her eyelashes brushed his cheek and Zyyr smiled softly. He moved slightly so that the tip of his nose nuzzled hers. His body was trembling slightly, but he wanted to savor every moment that he had with her. Each second, each breath was precious and he didn't want to hurry a single one of them. Their lips drew closer to each other and finally they touched. They melted into the kiss and Zyyr felt his soul reaching out to hers, seeking the connection that he so desperately wanted. As their mouths moved across each other Zyyr coaxed her lips apart with the tip of his tongue. She allowed them to open, welcoming his tongue in to explore her mouth more deeply.

Taking her by the waist, Zyyr eased backwards, drawing her with him as he laid back on the floor. He felt his erection press against her belly, her soft skin grazing across it so that intense sensations flowed through him. Lila pulled her mouth away from his and sat back so that she straddled him on her knees. Zyyr ran his hands up her thighs and over the swells of her hips to rest into the deep curve of her waist again. She began to rock her hips subtly, the movement causing the wet heat of her core to brush against his hardened shaft. He bit his bottom lip as his eyes closed and he focused in on the feeling of her body so close to his.

Zyyr felt Lila's hand flatten on the center of his chest just above his heart and he rested one of his over it.

"What are you thinking right now?" she asked breathlessly.

Zyyr opened his eyes and looked up at her. She was gazing down at him with a soft, irresistible blend of desire and innocence in her eyes.

"How incredible you are," he answered. "How much I want to slide inside of you right now."

Her hand tightened slightly on his chest and he felt the soft brush of her hair on his skin as she leaned forward to bring mouth close to his ear.

"Please, Zyyr," she whispered, her lips touching his ear as she spoke. "Make love to me."

"Are you sure?" he asked, his body aching for her now but not wanting to take advantage of her.

"Yes," she said. "I have heard rumors that the Denynso men are incomparable lovers."

Zyyr sat up sharply, grabbing Lila around the waist as he did so that he could continue to hold her close even without lying down.

"I don't want to be your lover, Lila," he said.

"You don't?" she asked, sounding both upset and embarrassed.

"No," he said. "I want to be your mate."

Her eyes widened and he nestled her a little closer, craving the closeness and needing her to be as focused as possible as he spoke to her. Even as many of the other warriors had spent their younger days bedding unbonded Denynso women prior to finding their mates, he had made the conscious and purposeful decision to not do that. The emotions that he was feeling were nothing like he had ever experienced, and he knew that this moment was everything that he had waited for. It would not just be another bedding that happened to result in his bond with his mate. This was something transcendent, powerful beyond even the words that he was trying to form for her, and he needed her to fully understand it.

"I don't want to claim just your body," he said, leaning forward to kiss the soft curve between her neck and her shoulder. He couldn't resist touching her. "I want to claim all of you. You were intended for me from the day of my birth and right now, in this moment, if you still want me, you will be devoting your life to me, and accepting the devotion of my life to you. You will be my mate, the most cherished of any person in my life, and there will be nothing that will ever come between us."

He realized that as he spoke his voice became quieter until he finished in nearly a whisper. When he was finished he looked up at her and saw a shifted emotion in the gaze she returned. The softness and affection had deepened now, creating something beautiful and intense that told him she had understood everything that he said to her.

"I would never want you to just be my lover," she whispered back. "I've known since I first saw you."

"Will you be my mate?" he asked.

Lila nodded, looping her arms around his neck and leaning forward to rest her forehead against his.

"Yes," she said.

Zyyr used the arm that was looped around her waist to lift Lila's hips and then lowered her down, sinking into her as he settled her into his lap. Her body was hot and tight around his cock and he heard her whimper slightly. Holding her still, he lifted his hips slightly so that he pressed deeper into her so that her body could become accustomed to holding him. Soon he felt her relax and her body open to him more so that he could press deeper still. Lila rolled her hips against his slowly and Zyyr felt a groan pour from his chest. Their bodies melded with indescribable perfection, creating a closeness that he could never have imagined. It felt as though her every curve was crafted to cradle him and his every hardened plane and sharp angle was designed to complement her softness.

Zyyr wrapped Lila's legs around his hips and tucked his own legs forward so that he held her tightly in his lap and she was fully engaged around him. He took her hips and changed their movement slightly, guiding then into a rocking motion that kept him buried deep within her but created long, deep strokes that had him feeling like he was rushing headlong into oblivion. Lila's head fell back and her back arched slightly, thrusting one taut pink nipple up toward him. Zyyr caught it in his mouth, drawing it in between his lips and nipping at it lightly with his teeth. He continued to suckle her as Lila rocked harder and faster against him. Her hands gripped at his back, digging harder into his skin the more passionate her pace became.

"Look at me," she suddenly gasped.

Zyyr pulled his mouth away from her breast and looked at her, catching her eyes. The instant that their gaze met, he felt the pleasure that had been swelling inside him spiral out of control. Pressure that had built through his thighs and stomach tightened even further until it was almost too much, and then released in a shattering climax. He felt his cock pulse and Lila cried out. Her body contracted around his, meeting each throb with a tightening of her own so that he could feel her milking him as he spilled into her.

He felt completely spent when the waves of his orgasm finally stopped. Lila's body draped over his, sweat making their skin slick and hot against each other. Zyyr held her as close as he could and kissed the top of her head, drawing in the scent of her hair. Everything had changed. The world was different now and he felt a greater sense of joy and fulfillment than he ever had. With that joy and fulfillment, however came a tremendous sense of responsibility. Lila was his, now, and it rested on his shoulders and in his heart to ensure that she was safe and protected no matter what type of threat she might face.

14

———

"Are you sure that you want to talk to her again?"

Maxim looked over at Ivy and nodded.

"I have to," he said. "Just one more time."

"She said that she doesn't want to talk about this."

"I know," Maxim said, "but I have to try one more time. Especially after everything that Athan told us, I have to give her one more opportunity to tell me what she knows, even if just to find out what she thinks happened and if there is anything that she might know that Athan didn't tell us."

"Why would Athan not tell you something? If he wanted to tell you what happened in the first place, especially with the threat that it poses to him, why would he hold anything back?" Ivy asked.

"It's not that I think that he would hold anything back," Maxim told her. "My father and mother were extremely close when he was here. I have never seen two people love each other the way that they did, and they were always whispering in their room. Athan was my father's best friend and he confided in him a lot, but I can see him not telling him everything, especially when it came to the Order, because of the turmoil within the organization and the always-present possibility that Athan could fall into line with the members of the Order who had transformed into being Klimnu."

"Do you really think that that was something that could have happened?" Ivy asked.

"I don't know," Maxim said. "That isn't a situation that I can even begin to imagine. I'm sure that Papa didn't want to think that Athan could ever betray him and the rest of our kind that way, but he also had to be cautious. He didn't know exactly what was happening or why, and he had to be suspicious of everyone. The only person who he could trust completely was my mother. She had nothing to do with the Order, so she would have no reason to use what he told her for any ulterior motive. I have a really hard time believing that he would hold all of that inside of him and wouldn't tell her anything at all. What if she knows something that even Athan doesn't?"

"She was surprised by what you told her, though, Maxim."

"Maybe. I have to at least ask her one more time."

"Maxim?"

Maxim turned to her and saw tears sparkling in Ivy's eyes. He reached forward and took her hands, pulling her closer so that she could feel the comfort of his body against hers.

"What is it, Ivy?" he asked.

"All of this is starting to scare me," she said.

"Why?"

"If the Order is so secretive that even Athan, one of the oldest and most respected members, is frightened of them finding out that they were talking to you, what do you think that they would do to us if they found out what he told us?"

"I will always keep you safe, my love. No matter what happens, you know that I am always here to protect you."

"What do you hope to accomplish with all of this, Maxim? Do you want to find your father's body? Do you want to find out who the members of the Order were that became Klimnu? I thought that we came back here because you wanted to know more about the Order, but now I don't know what good could possibly come of it."

"There is something that we don't know, Ivy. Something that even Athan doesn't know. My family deserves to know what happened to my father and why he would fight so hard. This can't just be as simple as he wanted to fight off the Klimnu and they killed him in battle. There has to be something else."

"Why?" Ivy asked. "Why does there have to be something else? Why couldn't it just be that simple? Why couldn't it just be that Aegeus found out about the Klimnu, knew that members of the Order had changed, he wanted to fight them off so that they couldn't threaten the rest of your kind, and the rogue members of the Order found out so they targeted him? If they were so determined to take over the planet, they would want to do whatever they could to prevent someone who was as powerful as your father from pushing them back. I just don't understand why you want to make it more complicated than that."

Maxim felt the words fall into his stomach like stones. He let her hands fall away from his and took a step back from her.

"You think that I want this to be this way?" he asked, feeling the pain in his throat that came from fighting the tears that had wanted to fall since he had returned to the kingdom. "You think that I am enjoying finding out all of this about my father?"

"Maxim," Ivy said, trying to reach for his hand, but he pulled away, "I'm sorry. I didn't mean to upset you. I just hate to see you this way. I wish that we could just put it all behind us and move on with our lives."

"Maybe you should stay out here while I talk to my mother," he said, turning away from her and stepping into the house.

Ivy hand touched the back of his shoulder as he walked away, but Maxim continued forward, letting her fingers run down his back and ignoring her voice as she called for him. He couldn't let himself focus on that pain in that moment. He couldn't allow himself to fall into her words and let the comfort that they offered to pull him away from the task that lay ahead of him. Maxim knew that he was doing what he had to do. His father would have wanted him to be strong and follow in his footsteps. It didn't make sense that he and Kyven weren't part of the Order. Though most of the contemporary Order was not hereditary, that was not the way that it used to be, and he couldn't help but wonder if part of the reason that they had been kept out of the tradition was to prevent them from ever finding out about what really happened to their father. If that was true, it meant even more than that he needed to find out what Aegeus had learned but had never told Athan and what had actually happened to him. If nothing else he would understand what had motivated his father in his last days and what he had envisioned for the world that his sons would grow up in.

He could only hope that soon Ivy would understand.

Ellora was standing in the kitchen braiding a loaf of bread on the counter when Maxim walked in.

"Hello, Maxim," she said.

Her voice sounded tired and worn, and for the first time Maxim let him think about his mother before Aegeus died.

She had been brighter, more energetic then. Her eyes had sparkled when she looked at him and there was light around her that seemed to carry her through everything she did. When his father died, that light faded. She was still kind, loving, and encouraging of him and of Kyven, but there was something missing. Over time he had put the thoughts of her before his father's death behind him, knowing even at that young age that things would never go back to the way that they were. He had resigned himself to the changed woman that his mother had become and eventually stopped thinking about those early childhood days. He couldn't help but think of them now, and he felt like they were stolen from him just as much as his father was.

"I need to talk to you," Maxim said.

Ellora stopped weaving the dough and hung her head, giving a deep sigh.

"Please, Maxim, don't start again. I already told you that I don't want to talk about any of this. It won't do any good."

"What do you know about the Klimnu? What did Papa tell you?"

"I don't know anything more than you do, Maxim. They used to be Mikana and then something happened to them and they changed. It had been happening for generations before your father became involved, but no one talked about it."

"What happened to get the Order involved?"

"I don't know, Maxim," Ellora said, going back to weaving the dough. "The number of Klimnu was becoming higher and they were getting more aggressive. I don't know why."

"And Papa didn't tell you anything at all about what he planned to do? You didn't know anything?"

"Where's Ivy?"

"She's outside. He didn't tell you anything?"

"What are you doing, Maxim?" she asked.

"What do you mean?"

"You are letting yourself get so wrapped up in the past that you aren't even looking into your future. Instead of thinking about that woman who obviously loves you, you are so determined to find out things that no one needs to know and that will do no one any good."

"I thought that you didn't want me to be with Ivy."

"I never said that, Maxim."

"You said as much."

"I'm sorry," Ellora said. "I am trying. Really I am. I just want you to be with someone who will make you happy, and who you can build a life with here."

"Right now all I am thinking about is Papa and finding out what happened. I can't even begin to think about having a future or a family if I don't even know my own history. He was doing something, Mama. He knew something and he had a plan to handle it, and something happened to him. That has impacted the entire planet since then, and I need to figure it out. If I have to do that without your help, that's what I'm going to have to do."

"I already lost my husband. I don't want to lose the rest of my family."

"If you know anything, you can help make sure that we stay safe."

"I don't know any more than what you already do. He wouldn't tell me anything. All I knew was that he was going into battle that day, but he assured me that he was going to be safe. He wasn't. He never came home. I don't know anything else."

15

Simran kept his back to the wall as he sipped the dark, earthy beer in his hand. It was similar to some of the drinks that they had on Uoria and it made him feel slightly homesick as he looked out over the party that was unfolding in front of him. It was yet another celebration of the wedding that would be happening in just a few days and he was starting to feel overwhelmed. The bonding of his kind on Uoria was something that happened quickly and only in the privacy of the space the two chose to share with one another. The marriage ritual of Earth, however, was complex and long, focusing far more on the people around the couple and their role in the community and their families rather than just the relationship of the couple itself. He wasn't sure how he felt about the contrast. As much as he liked the idea of friends and families having the opportunity to celebrate the union of two people, it somehow seemed that the union itself got lost among all of the parties, events, and preparations that he was witnessing.

Even as he thought this, his eyes wandered across the room to Jane. She had told him that this party was going to be different than the engagement party that they had hosted for Ty and Samira when they first arrived on Earth. While that party was more about toasting their plan to marry and letting friends and family greet and congratulate them, this party was about having the couple having fun before they "settled down". Simran wasn't entire sure what that was supposed to mean, but he went along with it, wanting to do anything that he could to spend more time with Jane.

Though he hadn't told any of the others yet, he had known since before they even landed that something incredible was going to happen to him during this visit to Earth. In the hours before the ship docked at the university he could feel the tension building in his belly and the heat starting to radiate off of his skin, telling him that his mate was waiting for him and that he would soon find her. He never would have expected to find his mate on Earth. Like the other Denynso warriors, it was just his assumption that he would find the partner who had been intended for him since birth among the women of his clan. Now as he looked at Jane, however, he knew that that was not the way that his life was going to happen.

He had done everything that he could to hide how he was feeling from the rest of the warriors and even from Jane. He knew that most of the warriors pursued their passion for their intended mate as quickly as they could from the moment that they found her. For some they completed their bond in a matter of hours. Though this created a strong, life-long connection between them just as it did for any pair of Denynso mates, it meant getting to know each other after they had already devoted themselves to one another. Simran struggled with the idea of finding that closeness with a woman that he didn't know, even though everything inside of him had compelled him to do just that since he first stepped off of the ship and met Jane.

He had spent the last several days with Jane, and the feelings that he had for her were almost overwhelmingly intense now. He knew now that the desire for her was more than just the urges of his body, but also the longing of his heart and his soul. Though his existence was so incredibly different than hers and he couldn't truly envision what it would mean to spend their lives together, he also couldn't imagine spending the rest of his life without her.

As if she could hear him thinking about her, Jane turned away from the women who she was talking with and smiled at him. She lifted the glass of sparkling wine in her hand like she was waving at him and he returned the gesture with his beer. Jane glanced back at the women and said something, one hand lifting to touch the arm of the woman in front of her. The woman nodded and Jane started across the room toward Simran. The warrior could feel his ever-present erection pressing toward her and was thankful for the tighter undergarments that he had put on so that she didn't notice as she approached him.

Her beautiful face grew brighter the closer she got to him, and when she was only a few steps away she glanced down like she was trying to hide the size of her smile.

"Hi," she said.

"Hi," he replied.

"Are you having fun?"

She took her place beside him, turning so that her back touched the wall like his did, and lifted her glass to her lips.

"Um," Simran said, looking out over the party again. "I think so." His eyes fell on a few of the women from the university climbing up on top of the bar and starting to dance, the men standing beneath them shouting and cheering. "Not as much as they are, I'm fairly sure, but fun, yes."

Jane laughed, pulling her glass away from her mouth and covering it.

"I don't think that anyone has ever had as much fun as they are," she said.

"It's kind of hard to envision any of those women working at the university," Simran said. "They don't exactly seem...academic."

"I wouldn't know," Jane said. "I don't know Samira from the university."

"That's right," Simran said, remembering what she had told him about her friendship with Jane. "I keep forgetting that you and Samira go further back than the university."

"Nope," she said, shaking her head as she watched the women stumbling across the top of the bar, "and that means that I don't get the joy of being a part of that delightful social group."

"Well, that's just a shame."

Simran laughed and nudged her with his elbow. Though the gesture was playful, it sent a tremble through his body. Jane seemed to feel something, too, because she looked up at him with slightly wider eyes and then looked down at her glass sharply.

"So, there's something else that not being a part of university has caused for me," she said.

Her voice was slightly softer now and the words came out almost cautiously, like she suddenly felt nervous about speaking to him.

"What is that?" he asked.

"I don't know much about you," she said.

"Me?" he asked.

"Your kind," she said by way of explanation. "Samira

mentioned learning about the Denynso a few times, and I know that there was an exchange program set up between the university and Uoria. That's all, though. I don't know anything else about the clan or even your planet."

The tone of her voice sounded like she was really telling him something else, but Simran wasn't sure what that could be.

"Is there something that you'd like to know?" he asked.

He took another sip of his beer as Jane turned to him and let her eyes travel across his face, following the curves of his jaw and then settling into his gaze. She stared at him for a few long moments.

"You remind me of something," she said.

"Of what?" he asked.

She shook her head and narrowed her eyes, staring deeper into him as if he was a filter allowing her to look into memories she couldn't quite touch.

"I don't really know. You just look so familiar, but I can't figure out why. You just remind me of something."

"I hope that it isn't anything bad," Simran said, trying to bring some levity into a moment that was feeling progressively more tense and heavy.

Jane made a sound like she was thinking through what she had said.

"I'm not sure."

16

"Maxim?"

Maxim turned toward Athan's voice and nodded at the man as he approached where Maxim was sitting on the wide back porch of Ellora's house.

"Hello, Athan."

"I came to tell you that I'm leaving."

Maxim stood sharply and took a step toward Athan.

"What do you mean you're leaving? Where are you going?"

"I don't know, but I can't stay here. Now that I've told you everything that I know about your father's death, it isn't safe for me to stay in the kingdom any longer. If the Order finds out, I will be targeted first."

"You can't just leave, Athan. You can't just walk away now."

"I have to, Maxim. It wasn't an easy decision to tell you everything that I have. I truly believed that I was going to bring all of that to my grave with me. When you came back here, though, I knew that that wasn't my choice to make.

What your father told me and what I experienced with him didn't belong to me. Those moments belonged to him, and that means they belong to you and to your mother. I struggled with telling you because of the danger that I knew even saying the words would create, but in the end it is something that I had to do. You deserved to know, and I believe that you will do with it what needs to be done."

"I need your help," Maxim insisted.

"No," Athan said. "You don't need me. I have done my part. There's nothing more than I can do for you."

Athan turned to leave and Maxim took another step forward.

"You owe this to him," Maxim said. "He trusted you. He might not have told you everything, but whatever it is that he chose to keep away from you, he did it for a reason. You know more than anyone, including my mother."

Athan turned back to look at him.

"Aegeus didn't tell your mother what was happening?" he asked.

"No. She only knew that you were going into battle that day and that Papa promised her that he was going to return safely. That's all. Anything else that you know and that you experienced is unique to you. You still hold all of those moments. You might have shared them with me, but that doesn't mean that they left you. You owe it to the trust that my father had in you and everything that you experienced with him to see this through. I understand that you are in danger, but so am I. All of us are now, Athan, and running isn't going to change that. They will come for you. They will find you. You say you didn't have a choice but to tell me what you knew. Now you don't have a choice but to stay and finish this for him."

Before Athan could respond Maxim heard loud foot-steps pounding toward them and the door to the porch swung open. Kyven and Emerie ran out onto the porch and Maxim saw the frantic look in his brother's eyes.

"Kyven," he said, walking around Athan toward his brother. "What is it?"

"You need to come with me," Kyven said.

Panic rose in Maxim's chest and he felt a sick feeling roll through his stomach.

"What is it? Is something wrong with Ivy?"

Despite the hurt and anger that still burned in his chest for her, his first thought was still to protect the woman who he deeply loved.

"No," Kyven said. "It isn't Ivy. Just come with me. You, too, Athan."

Maxim turned to look over his shoulder at Athan. The older man met his eyes and gave an almost imperceptible nod, offering his agreement to what Maxim had said. He nodded back and they followed Kyven back off of the porch and through their mother's house. He briefly thought that they were going out the front door, but Kyven suddenly turned and led them down a narrow hallway that held Aegeus's private rooms. These had been spaces that they had rarely been allowed to enter when they were younger and Maxim felt slightly uncomfortable entering them even now.

"I started thinking about these rooms and how much time Papa spent in them when we were younger," Kyven said as though responding to Maxim's thoughts. "He used to bring us to Athan's house and down into the tunnels, espe-cially you, but these rooms were off-limits most of the time. That made me think that there had to be something in here that was too dangerous for us to ever see."

"Why is she here?" Athan asked, pointing at Emerie.

Maxim saw Emerie's eyes flicker to Kyven and then her take a small step back like she was going to leave, but Kyven reached for her and took her hand.

"Because I asked her to be."

"This isn't the place for human women, Kyven," Athan scolded, but Kyven remained steadfast.

"She is not just a woman, Athan, and you don't have any authority to tell me who I can and can't be with. I'm not a child anymore and you don't need to keep trying to raise me in the place of my father."

The statement fell heavily and painfully around them and Athan took a step back.

"You're right," he said.

"What did you want to show us?" Maxim asked.

Kyven stepped into the second of the small cluster of rooms at the end of the hallway and the others followed him. He walked directly to a narrow door in the corner and opened it. Maxim stepped up close to the doorway and looked into the shallow closet. Kyven flattened his hand on the back wall and pressed. Maxim heard a click and then the wall moved aside, revealing a steep set of stairs leading down into darkness.

"What is this?" he asked.

Kyven looked back at him.

"There's more."

"You went down there?"

Kyven nodded. He reached into the pouch at his hip and withdrew a light stick, illuminating it as he handed it over to Maxim. Maxim took it and held it forward so that the light cut through the darkness of the stairs before starting down them. The air of the staircase was dense and thick. It felt like it carried all of the energy of the years that it had been closed and when Maxim filled his lungs with it he felt a surge of emotion rush through him.

"What is this, Athan?" he demanded.

"I don't know," Athan responded from behind him.

Kyven and Emerie had waited at the top of the stairs, allowing Maxim and Athan to go down first.

"You don't know?" Maxim asked.

"I promise you, Maxim. I have never seen this before. I don't know what this is or what's down here."

Maxim let his hand trail down the wall beside him as he walked down the stairs. He had gone down several steps when he felt the texture of the wall change. He paused and turned the light of the stick to the wall. His fingers followed the shape of a designed carved deeply into the wall and he felt a memory surfacing.

"This symbol," he said, looking back at Athan, "it has something to do with my grandfather."

Athan took another step down the staircase and leaned forward slightly to look at the design more closely. He nodded.

"It was his symbol within the Order," he said. "He must have built this."

"One of his hidden doors," Kyven said.

Maxim turned away from the symbol and continued down the stairs, keeping the light stick ahead of him to illuminate as much of the space as possible. Finally the walls beside him opened and he stepped off of the stairs into what looked like a small, low bunker. When Kyven joined him in the room he touched a panel on the wall beside him and the space filled with light. On the wall in front of him Maxim saw a larger version of his grandfather's symbol painted in gold across a black field. Just beneath it was another symbol painted in silver.

"Do you recognize that symbol?" Athan asked.

"It's my father's," Maxim said. "Kyven, is this what you wanted to show me?" he asked.

Kyven walked past them and Maxim watched as he lifted his hand to touch the symbol that represented their father. For a moment he thought that he was simply touching the shape to feel closer to Aegeus just as he wanted to do, but after a few seconds Kyven drew his hand down from the shape to a section of the wall just beneath it and pressed with his fingertips. A sound behind him made Maxim turn sharply. In the back corner of the room a section of the wall had shifted and moved aside, revealing another doorway.

Maxim crossed to the open section of the wall and looked in. He stepped into the short passageway and immediately the ceiling began to glow much like the tunnels beneath the kingdom. He moved down the passageway as quickly as he could, feeling like he was chasing the light as it glowed briefly above him and then extinguished as it lit up the section in front of him. He felt like he had only gone a few yards when the passageway ended and he found himself in another room, this one even smaller than the first. He stopped in the middle, the breath feeling like it had been torn from his chest and his heart beginning to beat so hard that he could hear the rush of his blood in his ears.

All around him the walls of the room were covered in weapons and armor. He turned slowly, trying to take it all in, trying to make sense of what he was seeing. Athan, Kyven, and Emerie came into the room with him, but he didn't acknowledge them. Instead, he reached forward and ran his fingertips along the edge of one of the long swords suspended on the wall with thick, heavy nails. Even after all of the years that had passed since Aegeus had stepped into that room, the edge of the weapon was still sharp enough to sting on his skin.

"What is this?" Maxim asked, repeating the question that he had asked when they first entered the stairwell, but now directing it to no one in particular. He was answered only by silence and he whipped around to look at the others in the room. "What is this?" he demanded.

"This is how I found it," Kyven told him.

"How did you find it?" Maxim asked.

"It was an accident," Kyven told him. "I went into the room just to see what was there. I thought that maybe I could find something that would help us. When I opened the closet, I noticed that the wall looked too close to the door, like the closet was too small. I touched it and it opened."

"How did you know to open the passageway to this room?"

"I just wanted to touch Papa's symbol," Kyven said softly, affirming what Maxim had felt when he first saw the shape on the wall. "I hadn't seen it in so long. Mama took all of them out of the house after he died and—" his voice trailed off and he took a breath, "I just wanted to feel close to him again."

"Why is all of this still here?" Athan asked, his voice low. "Why wasn't it with him?"

Maxim turned to him, struck by the question that he seemed to be asking himself rather than them.

"What do you mean?" he asked.

Athan looked up at him with questions lingering in his gaze.

"If he built this bunker and prepared it for war, why didn't he bring the weapons and armor with him when he went to war? When we walked into that battle, he only had one sword with him. He went to all of the trouble to build this, but then when he went to face down the enemy, he had nothing."

"What did it look like?" Maxim asked.

"What?" Athan asked.

"His sword. What did it look like?"

"It was just a sword. Just like the ones that the rest of us carried."

"Was it my grandfather's?"

"It might have been."

"My mother always told us that whenever he left home to do something with the Order, he carried my grandfather's sword."

"That's true. It's what he always had with him, so it must have been what he had that day."

"Where is it now?" Maxim asked and watched as Athan's eyes widened slightly, but he didn't respond. "Athan? Where is my grandfather's sword?"

"I don't know," Athan finally replied.

"Had he drawn it before he died?" Maxim asked.

Athan nodded and Maxim watched him walk up to the wall so that he could touch the same sword that he had.

"Yes," Athan said. "He stepped out onto the field and drew his sword. The last thing I saw was him pull it back as the Klimnu descended on him."

"Then he was gone."

"Yes."

"So where is the sword?"

"The Klimnu and their allies could have destroyed his body," Kyven said, "but they couldn't make a sword disappear completely. There would have been something left."

"Did you seen any part of it when you went back to the field to look for his body?" Maxim asked.

Athan turned away from the wall and met Maxim's gaze. "No."

TBC

(To be continued in book VII...)